The Billionaire's Club

Meet the world's most eligible bachelors...
by
Rebecca Winters

For tycoons Vincenzo Gagliardi,
Takis Manolis and Cesare Donati,
transforming the Castello di Lombardi into
one of Europe's most highly sought-after hotels
will be more than just a business venture—
it's a challenge to be relished!

But these three men,
bound by a friendship as strong as blood,
are about to discover that the chase is only half
the fun as three women conquer their hearts
and change their lives for ever...

Return of Her Italian Duke
Available now!

And look out for Takis and Cesare's stories
coming soon!

Dear Reader,

Some of you who have read my books in the past know I've always had a passion for the adventure stories of the great French writer Alexandre Dumas. *The Man in the Iron Mask* and *The Count of Monte Cristo* are two of my favourites!

Once again I've written a novel in which his brilliant storytelling has inspired me to write another version of *The Count of Monte Cristo*—Rebecca Winters style! It just happened without my realising it. That shows what a great influence he has had on me as a reader and a writer over the years.

I hope all of you will read with fascination *Return of Her Italian Duke*. It's the love story of the gorgeous Vincenzo Nistri Gagliardi, Duca di Lombardi, and his childhood sweetheart Gemma. After his eleven-year disappearance, how will she handle seeing him again? How would *you*?

Enjoy!

Rebecca Winters

RETURN OF HER ITALIAN DUKE

BY
REBECCA WINTERS

First Published in Great Britain 2017
By Mills & Boon, an imprint of HarperCollins*Publishers*
1 London Bridge Street, London, SE1 9GF

© 2017 Rebecca Winters

ISBN: 978-0-263-06851-1

Our policy is to use papers that are natural, renewable and recyclable
products and made from wood grown in sustainable forests. The logging
and manufacturing processes conform to the legal environmental
regulations of the country of origin.

Printed and bound in Great Britain
by CPI Antony Rowe, Chippenham, Wiltshire

Rebecca Winters lives in Salt Lake City, Utah. With canyons and high alpine meadows full of wildflowers, she never runs out of places to explore. They, plus her favourite vacation spots in Europe, often end up as backgrounds for her romance novels—because writing is her passion, along with her family and church. Rebecca loves to hear from readers. If you wish to email her, please visit her website at cleanromances.com.

Books by Rebecca Winters

Mills & Boon Romance

The Vineyards of Calanetti

His Princess of Convenience

The Montanari Marriages

The Billionaire's Baby Swap
The Billionaire Who Saw Her Beauty

Greek Billionaires

The Millionaire's True Worth
A Wedding for the Greek Tycoon

The Greek's Tiny Miracle
At the Chateau for Christmas
Taming the French Tycoon
The Renegade Billionaire
The Billionaire's Prize

Visit the Author Profile page at millsandboon.co.uk for more titles.

To my darling daughter Dominique, a wonderful romance writer who has an editor's instinct and insight to keep her mother's writing on track and believable.

She too is a Dumas lover.
We're both Francophiles at heart.

CHAPTER ONE

Castello di Lombardi, ten years ago

AT TWO IN the morning, Vincenzo Gagliardi, newly turned eighteen, quickly dressed in jeans and a hoodie he pulled over his black hair. The long sleeves covered the bruises on his arms. He could feel the welts still smarting on his back and legs as he slid his pack over his shoulders. Then he looked around his room one more time, glancing at the bed.

A vision of Gemma, the woman who'd been entwined in his arms there the night before, wouldn't leave his mind. After the pleasure they'd given each other despite his wounds, and the plans he'd envisioned for their future, it killed him to think he had to leave her at all. But the difficulties with his father made his flight necessary. Worse, he couldn't tell her where he was going or why. It was for her own protection.

Once his father, the acting Duca di Lombardi, started looking for him, he'd interrogate everyone, including Gemma, and he would be able to tell if she was lying or not. If the girl he'd grown up with from earliest childhood knew nothing about his disappearance, then his father would sense it and have to believe her.

Arrivederci, Gemma, his heart moaned. *Ti amo.*

Making sure no one saw him, he hurried through the fourteenth-century *castello* to Dimi's room in the other tower. His cousin had left his bedroom door open. Closer than brothers, they'd been planning Vincenzo's disappearance for a year.

Dimi was waiting for him. "You're late and must go now! I've been watching from the parapet. The guard with the dog won't be walking past the entrance for another seven minutes."

"This is it, cousin. Remember—when I'm established in New York, I'll contact you. Look for the phone number through an ad in the help wanted of *Il Giorno*'s classified section. Be sure to call me on a throwaway phone."

Dimi nodded.

"It won't be long before you turn eighteen. I'll wire you money so you can join me. And as soon as I reach my destination, I'll phone our grandfather so he won't worry." Both boys were the grandsons of the cancer-stricken Emanuele Gagliardi, the old Duca di Lombardi, who no longer could function and verged on death.

His cousin's eyes teared up. "*Che Dio di benedica*, Vincenzo."

He tried to clear his throat. "God be with you, too, Dimi. Promise me you'll keep an eye on Gemma."

"You know I will."

Vincenzo hated this situation that took him away from her, but there was no going back. He thanked his cousin for his sacrifice, hating their gut-wrenching separation and the horrible position he'd been put in. But they both agreed the danger was too great to do anything else.

As they hugged hard, Vincenzo realized that he could barely see through the tears. The deep well of shame and pain because he hadn't been able to protect his mother was something he would have to carry for the rest of his life. Gemma was better off without him.

Because of Dimi's loyalty, no one would ever know where he'd gone. This was the way it had to be.

Now that Vincenzo had been forced to cut himself off from the world he knew, the need to make money had taken hold of his life and had become his raison d'être.

Gemma lay in bed, wide-awake, at six in the morning, reliving the moments she'd spent with Vincenzo the night before last. When she'd heard he'd suffered injuries from a fall off his horse, she hadn't been able to resist slipping up to his tower bedroom to see if he was all right.

Despite his physical pain, they'd tried to love each other until he'd told her she needed to get back to her room. Gemma had wanted to stay the entire night with him and couldn't understand why he'd been so insistent she leave. She'd wanted to lie in his arms forever.

It was painful to have to tear herself away from him. After making sure no guards were watching, she slipped down the winding staircase at the back of the *castello* to reach the rooms where she and her mother lived behind the kitchen.

Yesterday after school she hadn't seen him at all,

and she feared his injuries were worse. If she didn't spot him in the back courtyard today after she got home, she'd go up to his room again tonight to find out why.

He was such an expert rider, it was hard to believe he'd been hurt so badly. While she suffered over what had happened to him, she heard a knock on her bedroom door. "Gemma? Get up and get dressed, then come in the main room quickly!"

She didn't normally get up until six thirty to start getting ready for school. Alarmed by the concern in her mother's voice, Gemma did her bidding.

When she emerged from the small room, she saw a sight she'd never forget. Vincenzo's father, the acting Duca di Lombardi, stood there while three policemen searched their rooms off the *castello* kitchen.

He and Vincenzo bore a strong likeness to each other, but there was all the difference in the world between them. The *duca*'s stare at her was so menacing, she shuddered.

Her mother grabbed her hand. "The *duca* wishes to ask you a few questions, Gemma."

He'd never talked to her personally in her life. "Yes, Your Highness?"

"Where's my son?"

She blinked. "I—I don't know what you mean," she stammered.

"If you know anything, you must tell him, Gemma."

"I know nothing, Mamma."

The police reappeared, shaking their heads. The *duca* took a threatening step toward her. "My son is missing from the *castello*, and I believe *you* know where he's gone."

Gemma froze. Vincenzo was gone? "I swear on my faith in the Holy Virgin that I have no idea where he would be."

His face turned a ruddy color. He shot a fiery glance at Gemma's mother, who crossed herself. "She's lying! Since you can't get the truth from her, I insist you leave the premises immediately and take your baggage with you." Gemma flinched. "I'll make certain you're never able to get another job again!"

He wheeled around and left. The police followed and shut the door.

Gemma ran to her mother and hugged her hard. Both of them trembled. "I swear I don't know anything about Vincenzo. I swear it, Mamma."

"I believe you. Start packing your bag. I'll do the same. We have to get out of here as soon as possible in case he comes back. I'll call for a taxi from the kitchen. We'll leave for the train station and go back to Florence."

Fifteen minutes later they assembled in the kitchen. The other cook and her daughter, Bianca, Gemma's best friend, were there, too, with their bags. The *duca*'s fury knew no bounds. As they hurried out of the service entrance at the back of the *castello* to wait, the *duca*'s words rang in her ears.

She's lying! Since you can't get the truth from her, you must leave the premises immediately and take your baggage you. I'll make certain you're never able to get another job again!

When the taxi arrived, Gemma climbed inside feeling as dead as last winter's ashes.

New York City, six months ago

After Dimi had phoned Vincenzo during the night with news that had come close to sending him into shock, he made calls to his two best friends and asked them to come to his Manhattan penthouse above his office ASAP.

Once arrangements were made, he told his assistant he wouldn't be in the office today and didn't want to be disturbed for any reason. Within two hours they'd both shown up using his private elevator.

The ultra-contemporary apartment suited Vincenzo perfectly. He liked the modern art on the white walls and the floor-to-ceiling windows that let in the light. Up here there were no dark reminders of the past. Here, he could breathe. Or he'd thought he could, until Dimi's phone call.

"Thanks for coming so fast," he said in Italian. "I'm just thankful you were available."

Cesare nodded. "You made it sound like life or death."

"It is to me."

His friend Takis eyed him curiously. "What's going on, Vincenzo?"

"Something that will surprise you. I'll tell you over breakfast. Come to the dining room."

Once they sat down and started to eat, Vincenzo handed them each a photograph of the massive Castello di Lombardi. "You're looking at the former residence of the Gagliardi family. From that family, two hundred years ago, sprang the first illustrious Duca di Lombardi, an important political figure in that region of Italy."

They stared at the photo, then looked at him in confusion.

"Why am I showing you this?" He read their minds. "Because there's more to me than you know. What I'm about to tell you could cause you to distrust me. You would have every right to walk out of here and never look back."

"Tell us what?" Cesare asked in total bewilderment.

"I haven't been completely honest about myself. You know me as Vincenzo Nistri, but my full name is Vincenzo Nistri Gagliardi. Nistri was my mother's maiden name."

Takis blinked. "So you're full-fledged Italian? For some reason you remind me of one of my Macedonian friends."

"That's what I thought, too," Cesare said. "Maybe Eastern Europe."

"Is that so?" Vincenzo grinned, amused by their honesty. "Not that I know of. The *castello* you're looking at was my home for the first eighteen years of my life." *And the woman I left behind there so cruelly is still the only girl I ever loved, though there've been women since.* "If a great tragedy hadn't happened to my family—one that caused me to flee—I would have taken over as the next Duca di Lombardi upon my father's death."

There was no question that he'd stunned his friends. Neither of them said a word. They kept staring at him as if he were an alien being speaking an unknown language.

"Let me tell you a story so you'll understand everything. My father and uncle did very bad things, evil things. At one point I realized my life was in danger."

When he'd given them details, he said, "The old *duca*, my grandfather, died nine years ago, leaving the way open for my father and uncle to bring down the house of Gagliardi. To start paying their debts, they sold off family treasures, including other properties that had been in the family for hundreds of years. Inevitably they let go the staff who'd served our family faithfully.

"Then a month ago my father was riding his horse through the forest behind the *castello* in a drunken rage. The horse reared and my father fell, breaking his neck. That left my uncle, Alonzo in charge.

"He has just been sent to prison, where he's now serving a thirty-year sentence for manslaughter, drunkenness, embezzlement and debt in the millions of euros. The family has now disintegrated, and the authorities have closed up the *castello*."

His friends shook their heads. "How could such a thing happen to a powerful family like yours?" Takis asked.

"There's one word for it. Corruption. Absolute and truly terrible. The family coffers had been raided for so long there was nothing left but staggering debt they'd accrued. They were like two bad seeds.

"My maternal grandparents died two years ago, and the only remaining family members on my father's side besides my imprisoned uncle are my cousin Dimi, who is like a brother to me, and his mother, Consolata. They live in a small palazzo in Milan given to her by her grandmother before her marriage to my uncle."

It was the only piece of property that neither Alonzo nor Vincenzo's father had been able to lay his hands on at the end.

"Dimi lives there quietly with her because she's in a wheelchair, suffering from dementia, and needs care." He eyed them directly. "Can you forgive me for omitting all of this until now?"

"*Si*—" both men said in unison. Takis's brows met. "Your life was in grave danger."

"But that's in the past. Now I'm faced with something I hadn't imagined, and I wanted to discuss it with you."

Cesare's solemn gaze played over him. "Tell us."

"The *castello* is now in receivership. I swore to God I would never return to Italy, but the thought of my heritage being sold to some foreign potentate to help the slipping Italian economy is anathema to me.

"My cousin Dimi is particularly concerned. He has an eye on what's happening everywhere. Both Italy's Villa Giulia museum in Rome, built by Pope Julius III, and the nine-hundred-year-old Norman palace in Palermo, the seat of former kings, are soon to be on the list to be sold off by the government, too.

"In view of such a frightening prospect, I wondered if you might like to go into business with me. Dimi will assist behind the scenes. Not only will my cousin and I be able to preserve our own family heritage, we'll transform the *castello* into a glorious hotel with a restaurant that could be the toast of Europe. It would mean the three of us would have to put our assistants in charge of managing our businesses when we're not in the country."

After a pronounced silence, both men let out cries

of excitement. For the rest of the day the three of them brainstormed.

"Now that we've talked things out, there's one favor I must ask. I intend to be the silent business partner in this venture and prefer to remain anonymous because of the family scandals."

Their solemn acknowledgment of his request warmed him and he knew they'd honor his request.

"Now, you can imagine that when word gets out that the *castello* has been sold and turned into a resort by two businessmen from the US, the press will be all over it. Dimi will send me the necessary information and put you in touch with the contact person to get the ball rolling.

"If we do decide to go into business together, I'll expect you two to do the negotiating. Naturally I'll supply the money needed so we can get started on the renovations right away."

Cesare smiled. "The *duca*'s return."

"No, Cesare. I don't want my title mentioned. That's not for public consumption." He couldn't escape the title he'd inherited by being his father's son, but in time he intended to renounce it legally through the court system. *And I'll find Gemma if it kills me.* Over the last ten years, no search had turned up any evidence of her.

"Understood." Cesare eyed him seriously. "When we first met at university, I always knew there was a lot more to you, but I couldn't put my finger on it and didn't dare ask for fear of insulting you."

"Now it's all making sense," Takis admitted. "Your English is too perfect, and you're far more sophisticated and knowledgeable than anyone else I know."

"Your friendship has meant the world to me. Let's hope for success in our new venture."

Takis sat back in the chair. "Edmond Dantes had nothing on you, Vincenzo Gagliardi."

Florence, Italy, present day

The bulletin board of the Florentine Epicurean School of Hospitality and Culinary Arts listed the latest career openings across four continents for their recent graduates to investigate.

At twenty-seven years of age, Gemma had finally received her long-awaited certification with the much-coveted first-place blue ribbon, and she hurried down the corridor toward the office. Everyone wanted to apply for the most prestigious position posted. She didn't know what her chances were, but it didn't matter. Her hard, grueling years of schooling were over, and she would find a position that guaranteed her a new life so she could prove herself.

She wanted to pay back her mother's family, who'd taken them in after they'd been thrown out of the Castello di Lombardi. Her relationship with Vincenzo years ago had put her family in such dire straits, it had ruined her mother's career. Gemma felt the responsibility heavily, because she hadn't heeded her mother's warnings that a commoner didn't mingle with royalty. But those days were behind her.

With students gathered around the bulletin board, it was hard to get close enough to write down the information. Later the lists would be put online, but she was too impatient and took pictures of the various announcements with her cell phone.

Her best friend Filippa Gatti, who'd gone through pastry school with Gemma, had the same idea. They made plans to talk later before she hurried off. Gemma found a bench farther along the corridor and sat down to study everything but gave up because she couldn't concentrate with so much noise.

Once outside, she got in her old blue car and headed back to her aunt's apartment two miles away. Her mother's sister owned the hundred-year-old Bonucci family bakery and ran it with her married daughter. When Gemma and her mother had fled to Florence, her aunt had let them live in the apartment above the bakery.

Her aunt was goodness itself and had put her mother to work. She had also helped Gemma get a scholarship to attend cooking school, because her mother's funds were so low. Her cousin was wonderful, too, and they all got along.

Once she had started culinary school, Gemma had helped out in the bakery every day after classes. The culinary school required ten years of apprenticeship. After high school she'd begun her training there. Now that she'd graduated, it was important she start paying her aunt back for letting them live there and helping to get them on their feet after being kicked out of the *castello*.

Today she dashed up the back stairs to the door off the porch. Gemma couldn't wait to call her mom and aunt and tell them she'd been chosen the top graduate in her class. After they'd shown such faith in her, Gemma was thrilled that her hard work had paid off.

But of course, it would happen that her mother and aunt had just left to go on a well-deserved vacation to the United Kingdom with friends, their first in years. They wouldn't be back for three weeks, because their trip included England, Scotland, Wales and Ireland. Such good news from the school had filled Gemma with joy. She would have to phone her *mamma*, Mirella, immediately.

Now that she'd received her certification, she was anxious to find a fabulous job and move out. She planned for her mother to go with her. They'd find a small, affordable apartment. Her mother could stop working and enjoy her life while her daughter earned the living.

After grabbing her favorite fruit soda from the fridge, Gemma sank down on the chair at the small kitchen table and phoned her *mamma*. Frustrated when she got her voice mail, Gemma asked her to phone her back ASAP because she had exciting news.

Next, she scrolled through her photo gallery to the information she'd recorded on her cell. To her utmost disappointment, none of the eighteen openings for pastry chefs were in France, the place where she'd had her heart set on working.

Both the French and the Italians thought they produced the finest chefs. As her mother and aunt had told her, because she was a woman, she'd have an even harder time breaking into a top five-star restaurant in either country. Women chefs still struggled for equality. One day she would get a position on the Côte d'Azur. But for now she needed a job right away!

Trying to manage her disappointment, she studied each opening one at a time: five in Spain, three in England, one in Liechtenstein, two in Australia, three in Japan, three in Canada, one in Italy.

Since it couldn't be France, nothing else thrilled her, but she studied the requirements for the various openings.

It wasn't until she came to the last posting, from Italy, that Gemma was shaken to the core. She thought she'd read it wrong. The shock had her jumping up from the couch. She read the words again, attempting to quell the frantic pounding of her heart.

Location: Milan, Italy. Fourteenth-century castello and former estate of the deceased Duca di Lombardi, Salvatore Gagliardi. Grand opening of the five-star Castello Supremo Hotel and Ristorante di Lombardi, July 6.

July 6 was only four weeks away. She read on.

Résumés for executive chef and executive pastry chef are being accepted. See list of requirements. Only those with the proper credentials need apply.

Gemma came close to fainting when she thought of Vincenzo. The fact that he'd disappeared without even saying goodbye had caused an anger in her that, even now, she was still trying to suppress. He'd told her he was in love with her and that one day they'd find a way to be married.

After he'd vanished, she'd felt so used. What a fool she'd been to believe he could love the daughter of a cook! How naive of her to think the *duca*-to-be would consider an alliance with an underling like Gemma. In her dream world they'd been equals and anything was possible. But once Vincenzo's father had tossed her and her mother out like a heap of garbage, she'd received the wake-up call of her life. It had shaken her world forever.

As she read the announcement again, something twisted painfully inside her. The *castello*, an icon over the centuries that had been her home until the age of seventeen, had now been turned into a hotel and restaurant. She tried to understand how such a thing could have happened to the family with its succession of *duchi* for over two hundred years.

Gone was their birthright and traditions. Vincenzo had disappeared along with his family. Last year she'd heard on television that Vincenzo's father was dead. And soon after that Dimi's father had been sent to prison for fraud. Beyond that there'd been no more news.

Now she was horrified to think the *castello* had been put up and sold for its commercial value in an increasingly mercenary world. Gemma considered it a form of sacrilege.

No doubt every new graduate would apply there first, but they didn't have a prayer of being hired. Only the most famous chefs throughout Europe and elsewhere would be allowed an interview at such a magnificent and famous landmark. Many considered Italy to be the vortex of gastronomic delight in the world. The competition would be fierce.

Even so, she was going to apply.

After her failed relationship with Paolo, she realized she needed to draw a line under the past. Until she discovered what had happened to Vincenzo and why, she knew in her heart she'd never be able to move on with her life.

If by some miracle she only made it to the first interview before being rejected, maybe she'd be able to find out where Vincenzo had gone. What had caused the demise of the Gagliardi family? So much had been hushed up in the press.

Pushing those thoughts aside, for the rest of the day she emailed her prepared résumé to Milan, Valencia, Barcelona, London and Vaduz in Liechtenstein. For some reason she couldn't attach her picture, but it was too late to worry about that now.

Filippa called to tell her she'd applied for all three jobs in Canada. She would have preferred to go to the States, but Canada was the next closest place with openings. Gemma wished her luck and told her what she'd done. They promised to keep each other updated on what happened.

The next day she started receiving emails back and learned that the positions in Vaduz and Valencia had already been filled. Barcelona and London were still open. To her satisfaction, they'd sent her a specific day and time to report for a personal interview.

But it was the email that came after lunch from the *castello* that almost sent her into cardiac arrest. She was told to report there at noon tomorrow! And to please let them know immediately if she couldn't make it.

Gemma had thought, of course, that being a new graduate, she wouldn't have been considered. Something on her résumé must have caused them to give her an opportunity.

Thank heaven her mother wasn't in Italy right now.

Gemma needed to see this through before she told her parent anything. The last thing she wanted to do was hurt her *mamma*. But for Gemma's own emotional health and progress, she had to do this! It might be her only chance in this life to find out about Vincenzo. If she didn't follow through, she knew she'd always regret it.

With hands trembling, she sent an email to let them know she'd be there at the correct time. If she left Florence within the hour, she could drive to the village at the base of the *castello* today and find a room for the night. That would give her time tomorrow to get ready before the interview.

Gemma phoned her cousin to let her know that she was leaving for a day or two to go job hunting. She made no mention that her destination was the *castello*. Her cousin had been so hurt for Gemma and her mother, she would have tried to persuade her to avoid more pain and not go. But this was something she had to do.

Without wasting any time, she showered and packed a suitcase that included her laptop. After dressing in jeans and a blouse, she set off on the three-hour drive to Milan full of questions that might get answered after all this time. It would be a trip of agony and ecstasy, since she'd never once been back.

By seven in the evening, she'd arrived in the busy city and took the turnoff for the village of Sopri, where she'd gone to school with a few children of the other estate workers. Even after all this time, Gemma knew where to find a *pensione* with reasonable rates.

But sleep didn't come well. She tossed and turned

for hours. Memories of Vincenzo and the night they'd been together in his bedroom kept her awake. Lying in his arms she'd felt immortal, but he hadn't let her stay with him all night, something she'd never understood.

How she'd loved her life at the *castello* with him! For years since his disappearance she'd tried to discover his whereabouts, but he'd vanished as if into thin air. Over time it finally sank in that she hadn't been good enough for him. That's what her mother had been trying to tell her without putting the painful message into actual words. Gemma believed it now!

When she wasn't hating Vincenzo, she feared that something terrible had happened to him. The possibility that he might have died was insupportable to her. Combined with her pain over the loss of Vincenzo was her outrage for what his father had done to her and her beloved mother. The great, cruel Duca di Lombardi! There were times when the memory of that morning still tormented her.

Once they'd moved to Florence, she'd never heard anything about Vincenzo or Dimi. Where had his cousin gone? She'd once hoped that if she could even find Dimi, she'd get answers to all her questions. But it was as if the Gagliardi family had been erased from life. It was too strange... She missed Dimi. He'd been such a wonderful friend all those years ago.

Now she was going back to the place where she'd known such joy...and pain. What if by some stretch of the imagination she got the job? How would she feel? How would her mother feel to realize her daughter had graduated with honors from the top cooking school in Italy and was going to make it despite what the *duca* had done to them?

Wouldn't it be the height of deliciousness to be hired there, of all places on earth? Such sweet revenge after being kicked to the gutter.

Gemma was relieved when morning came. After washing her hair and showering, she dressed in a peach-colored two-piece suit, wanting to look her best. At ten she ate breakfast at a trattoria before leaving for the *castello* ten minutes away. She'd planned to get there early enough to look around and ask questions. Surely someone would be able to tell her about Vincenzo.

For him to disappear on her was a betrayal so awful, she hadn't been able to put her trust in another man for years. Even after she'd starting dating, the memory of that horrible time when it became clear he'd never be back still haunted her nights.

It had taken until a year ago for her to have her first serious relationship with a man. After a month of dating, Paolo wanted to sleep with her, but she couldn't. Her heart wasn't in it. She explained to him that in another eight months she'd be graduating and looking for a position, hopefully in France. There could be no future for them. She had to follow her own path.

After breakfast Gemma opened the car window and breathed in the warm June air as she drove past the familiar signposts, farms and villas toward the massive Castello di Lombardi.

The ocher-toned structure, with its towers and crenellated walls sprawled over a prominent hilltop, had its roots in ancient times. So many nights she and

Vincenzo had walked along those walls with their arms around each other, talking and laughing quietly so none of the family or guards would see or hear them.

Closer now, cypress trees bordered her on either side of the winding road. Memories came flooding back. Because of Vincenzo, she knew all about its history. The remains of a Romanesque church standing in the inner courtyard dated back to AD 875. But the *castello* itself had been built in the fourteenth century to protect the surrounding estate from invasions.

Many owners had possessed it, including the House of Savoy. By the mid–eighteen hundreds it had become the residence of the Gagliardi family. Although it was the first Duca di Lombardi who was considered illustrious, as far as Gemma was concerned that right would have belonged to Vincenzo. That was, until he'd plunged a dagger in her heart by disappearing.

The visitor parking beneath the four flights of zigzagging front steps held no cars. Her breath caught to see the profusion of flowers and landscaping done to beautify everything. New external lighting fixtures had been put in place. At night it would present a magnificent spectacle to guests arriving.

After taking it all in, she drove down a private road that wound around to the rear entrance where in the past the tradesmen used to come. Beyond it was a large parking area that she remembered had been used by the staff.

There were a dozen vans and trucks, plus some elegant cars, clustered in the enclosed area around the door. From the front of the *castello* the entire place had looked deserted, but that clearly wasn't the case.

Once she'd gotten out of her car to walk around, a male gardener planting flowers called to her. "The lady is lost, perhaps?" he asked in Italian.

She shook her head. *Anything but.* "I'm here for a job interview."

"Ah? Then you must go around to the front. The office is on the right of the entrance hall."

"Thank you." It seemed that the day room she remembered must have been converted into an office. She could never have imagined it. "Tell me—do you know why the *castello* was sold in the first place?"

He hunched his shoulders. "*No lo so.*"

With her hair swishing against her shoulders, Gemma nodded and walked back to her car, realizing she'd get nothing from him. Her watch said eleven forty-five. She might as well arrive a few minutes early to show she was punctual. She backed her car around, retracing her short trip back to the main parking lot, where she stopped the car and got out.

How many hundreds of times had she and her childhood friend Bianca—who'd had a crush on Dimi—bounded up these steps after getting off the school bus looking for Vincenzo and his cousin?

They would enter the *castello* through a private doorway west of the main entrance and hurry down the corridor to the kitchen. Once they'd checked in with their mothers, they'd run off to their hiding place in the back courtyard, where hopefully the two Gagliardis would be waiting.

To her surprise the old private entrance no longer existed. The filled-in stone wall looked like it had been there forever. Gemma felt shut out and could well believe she'd dreamed up a past life.

But when she entered through the main doors, she had to admit that whoever had undertaken to turn this into a world-class resort had done a superb job of maintaining its former beauty. Many of the paintings and tapestries she remembered still adorned the vaulted ceilings and walls on the right side of the hallway.

The biggest difference lay in the bank of floor-to-ceiling French doors on the left. They ran the length of the long hallway she used to run through on her way to the kitchen. Beyond the mullioned glass squares she could see a gorgeous dining room with huge chandeliers so elegant it robbed her of breath.

On the far side of the dining room were more French doors that no doubt opened on to a terrace for open-air dining. Gemma knew there was a rose garden on that side of the *castello*. And though she couldn't see it from here, there was a magnificent ballroom beyond the dining room to the south.

She was staggered by the changes, so exquisite in design she could only marvel. Whoever had taken over this place had superb taste in everything. Suddenly she realized it was noon and she swung around to report she was here.

The enormous former day room had been transformed into the foyer and front desk of the fabulous hotel, with a long counter, several computers and all the accoutrements essential for business. She sat down on one of the eighteenth-century sage-and-gold damask chairs with the Duca di Lombardi's royal crest and waited to see if someone would come.

Just as she was ready to call out if anyone was there, she saw movement behind the counter that revealed an attractive brown-haired male, probably six foot two and in his late twenties. Strong and lean, he wore trousers and shirtsleeves pushed up to the elbows. When his cobalt-blue eyes wandered over her, she knew he'd missed nothing.

"You must be Signora Bonucci."

CHAPTER TWO

GEMMA CORRECTED HIM. "I'm Signor*ina* Bonucci."

"Ah. I saw the ring."

"It was my grandmother's." Gemma's mother had given it to her on her twenty-first birthday. Her grandmother had also been a great cook, and the hope was that it would bring Gemma luck. Now Gemma wore it on her right hand in remembrance.

As for the name, Bonucci, that was another story. Once Gemma and her mother had left the *castello*, Mirella had insisted Gemma use her maiden name. She'd hoped to be able to find work if the *duca* couldn't trace them through her married name, Rizzo.

One corner of his mouth lifted in a smile. "Now that we have that straightened out, I'm Signor Donati, the one who's late for this meeting. Call me Cesare." With that accent the man was Sicilian down to his toenails. "Thank you for applying with us. Come around the counter and we'll talk in my office."

She got up and followed him down a hallway past several doors to his inner sanctum, modern and in a messy state. Everything about Cesare surprised Gemma, including the informality.

"Take a seat."

Gemma sat down on one of the leather chairs. "I have to admit I was surprised that you would even consider a new graduate."

He perched on the corner of his desk. "I always keep an open mind. I had already chosen the finalists and the field was closed, but when your résumé showed up yesterday, it caught my eye."

"Might I ask why?"

"It included something no one else's did. You said you learned the art of pastry making from your mother. That was a dangerous admission and made me curious to know why you dared." He was teasing her.

"It *was* dangerous, I know." For more reasons than he was implying, but the *duca* was dead now. "To leave my mother from my résumé would make me ungrateful."

She felt his gaze studying her. "For you to mention her means she wasn't just an average cook in your eyes."

"No. She came from a family of bakers. To me, her pastry will always be the best." Gemma owed her mother everything after her sacrifices.

The man cocked his head. "It shows you're willing to give credit where it's due. But being the daughter of a cook doesn't always make the daughter a cook, no matter the genes nor how many classes at school."

"No one is more aware of that than I am, but I would be nothing without her. She helped me go to cooking school in Florence."

He folded his arms. "The best in Italy, where you received the highest award during your ten year apprenticeship there. It's a stringent education, but the most prestigious culinary schools require that much training to turn out the best cooks. She guided you well. Bravo."

A compliment from a man who knew the culinary business well enough to be in charge of staffing this new hotel came as a complete surprise.

"If I hadn't been born her daughter, I would never in this world have decided on a career that keeps you on your feet all day and night, that will never pay enough money and that is unfair to women chefs in general. In truth I'm shocked you allowed me this interview, even if you are exceptionally open-minded."

She shouldn't have said it, but she'd spoken without thinking. Incredibly he burst into laughter.

"Signorina, you're like a breath of fresh air and have won yourself one chance to prove if there's genius in you. Report to me at ten in the morning and I'll put you to work making what you do best."

Gemma stared hard at him. "You're serious…" Was it really possible?

His brows lifted. "When it comes to cooking, I'm always serious. You'll be sharing the kitchen with another applicant who is hoping to become the executive chef. All the ingredients you need will be provided, and you'll both have your own workspace. When you're finished, you will leave. Any questions?"

Yes. She had a big one, but now wasn't the moment. It had to be another test to see how well two different chefs got along under this kind of pressure. "None, Signor."

"*Bene.* When your pastry has been sampled by the people in charge tomorrow evening, an opinion will be made. The next day you'll be phoned and informed of their decision. Please see yourself out."

Now she was scared. She'd heard back from her mother last night and had been able to tell her about receiving the top marks for her certification. Her mother and aunt had been overjoyed. Gemma had told them she planned to apply at quite a few places for work, but she'd left out the position offered at the *castello*.

There was no need for her mother to know about it since Gemma had no real hope of getting it. Instead she'd asked them about their trip and they'd talked for a long time. Her mother had sounded so happy, Gemma hadn't wanted to say anything to take away from her enjoying the only trip she'd had in years.

Deep in painful thoughts, Vincenzo strode down the portrait-lined *castello* hallway toward his deceased grandfather's private dining room. Even after being back in Italy for a half year, it was still hard to believe this had once been his home.

All Vincenzo could think about was Gemma. Over the last ten years, he'd paid an Italian private investigator to look for her to no avail. For the six months he'd been in Lombardi, he'd doubled the search. Vincenzo's guilt over how his unexplained disappearance must have hurt Gemma beyond description had tortured him from the beginning. It matched his fear that he would never catch up to her again.

Though Dimi had promised to keep an eye on Gemma for him, fate had stepped in to change Dimi's life, too. The day that Vincenzo's father had gone on a rampage over his disappearance and had searched the countryside for him with the help of Dimi's father and the police, Dimi had realized the danger in staying at the *castello*. That very morning he'd left with his mother and taken her to her family's property in Milan, where they'd be safe and out of the way.

On his own, Dimi had searched for Gemma, but that path had led nowhere, either.

The thought filled Vincenzo with such profound sadness, gripping him to the point he couldn't throw it off. Echoes and whispers from a time when he'd known real happiness with Gemma haunted him and made his disconnect with the past even more heart wrenching.

His friends looked up when he entered. They must have heard his footsteps on the intricate pattern of inlaid wood flooring. Before he sat down at the oval table, Vincenzo's silvery-gray eyes—a trait of the Gagliardi men—glanced at the wood nymphs painted on the ornate ceiling.

Twenty-eight-year-old Vincenzo found them as fascinating now as he'd done as a little boy. One of them had always been of particular interest, because Gemma could have been the subject the artist had painted.

"*Mi dispiace essere in ritardo.* I was on the phone with Annette."

The savvy real estate woman he'd been involved with before leaving New York had wanted to plan her vacation to be with him for the opening. Deep down he knew she was hoping for a permanent arrangement. But since Vincenzo had stepped on Italian soil, memories of Gemma had had a stranglehold on him. He knew he wasn't ready to live with anyone, let alone get married.

Maybe after the opening he'd be able to relax and give it more thought. He enjoyed Annette more than any woman in a long time. But he had work to do and had told her he would call her back when he had more time to talk. The disappointment in her voice when he said he had to hang up because he was late for a business dinner spoke volumes. It was the truth.

Cesare smiled at him. "*Non c'e problema.*"

Greek-born Takis grunted. "Maybe not for you, Cesare, but I didn't eat lunch on purpose, and now I'm famished."

Vincenzo nodded. "I held back, too. Tonight is the night we make decisions that will spell the success or failure of our business venture. Let's get started."

"Just so you know, a fourth pastry chef applicant has created a sampling of desserts for us this evening."

"A fourth?" Vincenzo frowned. "I thought we were through with the vetting process."

"I thought so, too, but this one came in at the last minute yesterday with amazing credentials, and I decided to take a chance."

Takis groaned. "So we have to eat two sets of desserts?"

"That's right, so don't eat too much of any one thing," Cesare cautioned them.

On that note Vincenzo used his cell phone to ring for dinner. Tonight was the final night in their search to find the perfect executive chef and executive pastry chef for their adventure. The right choices would put them on the map as one of the most sought-after resorts in the world.

They'd narrowed the collection of applicants down to three in one category and now four in the other, but they were cutting it close. In one month they would be opening the doors and everything would have to be ready.

Their recently hired maître d', Cosimo, came up on the newly installed elevator and wheeled in a cart from the kitchen with their dinner. If tonight's food was anything like the other two nights, they were in for a very difficult time choosing the best of the best. The battle between the finalists was fierce.

For the next half hour they sampled and discussed the main course and made the decision that the French applicant would become their executive chef.

With that accomplished, Vincenzo rang for the desserts. Cosimo brought in the tray of delicious offerings from the third pastry chef.

"Remember," Cesare reminded them, "we have one more round of desserts from the fourth pastry chef to sample." He passed them a dish of water crackers. "Eat a few of these now so you'll be able to appreciate what's coming." They drank tea with the crackers to help cleanse their palates.

Cosimo wheeled in the last offerings of the night. As he placed the tray on the table, Vincenzo took one look at the desserts and thought he must be dreaming. *All* of them were Italian, and there were so many of them! They made up the parts of his childhood. He couldn't decide what to try first.

Unaware of his friends at this point, he started on *sfogliatelli*, his favorite dessert in the world, layered

like sea shells with cream and cinnamon. When he'd
eaten the whole thing he reached for the puffed dome
of sweet panettone, the bread his family had eaten on
holidays. When he couldn't swallow another bite, he
lifted his head. His friends were staring at him like
he'd lost his mind.

Takis nudged Cesare. "I believe we've found our
executive pastry chef."

"But first we must get Vincenzo to a hospital. He's
going to be sick."

Their smiles widened into grins, but he couldn't
laugh. All these desserts were too good to be true
and tasted like the ones prepared by Gemma's mother
years ago. But that was impossible!

He eyed Cesare. "Who made these?"

"A graduate from the Florentine Epicurean culinary school."

Vincent shook his head. "I need to know more." At
this juncture his heart was thumping with emotion.

Their smiles receded. Cesare looked worried.
"What's wrong?"

"Tell me this person's name."

"Signorina Bonucci. I don't remember her first
name. It's on her résumé in my office."

The name meant nothing to Vincenzo. "How old
is she? Early sixties?" Had Mirella, Gemma's mother,
seen the advertisement and applied for the position?

"No. She's young. In her midtwenties."

How could anyone reproduce desserts identical
to Mirella's unless she knew her or had worked with
her? If that were true, then perhaps she could tell him
Gemma's whereabouts!

"What's going on, Vincenzo?"

For the next few minutes he told them about one of the cooks at the *castello* years ago. "Her pastry was out of this world. She had a daughter who was a year younger than me. We grew up together on her mother's sweets. She was my first love."

"Ah," they said in a collective voice, clearly surprised at another one of his admissions.

"I have no idea what happened to either of them. In fact, over the years I've spent a large sum of money trying to find them, with no success. I want to meet this applicant and find out how she happens to have produced the same desserts."

He jumped up from the chair and hurried out of the room to the elevator at the end of the hall. Once on the main floor, they walked through the lobby and congregated in Cesare's private office. His friend pulled up the résumé on his computer for Vincenzo, who stood next to him to read it.

Seeing her first name nearly gave him a heart attack.

Gemma Bonucci
Age: 27
Address: Bonucci Bakery, Florence Top student in the year's graduating class of pastry chefs.

He was incredulous. His search had come to an end. He'd found her!

Vincenzo had known her as Gemma Rizzo. So why Bonucci? So many questions were bombarding him, he felt like he'd been punched in the gut.

"This must be Mirella's daughter, but there's no picture of her."

"It wasn't attached to her application," Cesare explained, "but her cooking is absolutely superb."

"So was her mother's. I can't comprehend that she was in the kitchen earlier cooking our dessert."

"You look a little pale. Are you all right?"

Vincenzo eyed Cesare. "I will be as soon as I get over the shock. You don't know what these last ten years have been like, trying to find her and always coming to a dead end…"

"Do we agree she's our new executive pastry chef?" Takis asked.

Vincenzo looked at both men. "Don't let my overeating influence you in any way. I have a terrible Italian sweet tooth, but we need to consider the various preferences of all patrons who will come through our doors. I'm sorry that you haven't been able to vote your conscience because of my behavior."

"It wasn't your behavior that decided me," Cesare insisted. "That was the best tiramisu I've ever eaten."

"Don't forget the baba and the baby cannoli," Takis chimed in. "Every dessert was exquisite and presented like a painting. When the guests leave, they'll spread the word that the most divine Italian desserts were made right here."

"Amen." This from Cesare. "But Vincenzo, did you have to eat all the *sfogliatelli* before we could sample it? Cosimo had to bring us more. It was food for the gods."

It was. And the lips of the loving seventeen-year-old girl Vincenzo had once held in his arms and kissed had been as sweet and succulent as the cinnamon-sprinkled cream in the pastry she'd prepared for this evening.

"Takis will make the phone calls now and tell our two new chefs to come to the office at noon for an orientation meeting." Cesare's announcement jerked Vincenzo out of his hidden thoughts.

"I'm glad the decisions have been made. As long as I'm in your office, I'd like to see the résumés of the other pastry finalists." It was an excuse to take another look at Gemma's.

"Be my guest," Cesare murmured. "Those desserts finished me off. I may never eat again."

"You're not the only one. I'm going to my office to make the phone calls."

But for the stunning realization that tomorrow he would see Gemma—the chef who'd turned them all into gluttons—Vincenzo would have laughed.

He walked around the desk and sat down in front of the computer screen to look at it. Her training had been matchless. She held certificates in the culinary arts, baking and pastry, hospitality management, wine studies, enology, and molecular gastronomy. She'd won awards for jams, preserves, chocolate ice cream. Mirella's chocolate ice cream had been divine.

The statement she'd made to explain her desire to be an executive pastry chef stood out as if it had been illuminated. *I learned the art of pastry making from my mother and would like to honor her life's work with my own.*

His eyes smarted as he rang Cesare.

"*Ehi, come va*, Vincenzo?"

"Sorry to bother you. What was it about Signorina Bonucci's résumé that decided you on allowing her to compete? I'm curious."

"You know me. My *mamma*'s cooking is the best

in the world, and I never make a secret about it. When I read about her wanting to honor her *mamma*'s cooking, I decided it was worth giving her a chance. On a whim I told her to report to the *castello*. I did the right thing in your opinion, *non e vero?*"

He closed his eyes tightly. "You already know the answer to that question. If you'd ignored her application, I doubt I would ever have found her." His throat closed up with emotion. "*Grazie, amico.*"

"I'm beginning to think it was meant to be. Before I hang up, there's one thing you should know, Vincenzo."

"What's that?"

"I didn't tell you before because I didn't want you or Takis to think I was biased in picking her for personal reasons."

His pulse sped up. "Go on."

"The signorina is beautiful. Like the forest nymph on the dining room ceiling you were staring at tonight. You know, the one leaning against the tree?"

Yes. Vincenzo knew the one and felt his face go hot. One night when he'd been kissing Gemma, he'd told her she reminded him of that exact nymph painted in the room where Vincenzo had spent many happy times talking to his grandfather. Cesare had noticed the resemblance, too.

"*A domani*, Cesare."

"*Dormi bene.*"

Vincenzo turned off the lights and headed for his old bedroom in the tower. No renovations had been made here. Guests would never be allowed in this part of the *castello*. It was too full of dark memories to open to the public.

He removed his clothes and threw on a robe before walking out on the balcony overlooking Sopri at the foot of the hillside where he'd run away. Where was she sleeping tonight? Down below, near to where she'd once attended school? Or in Milan?

Vincenzo knew her deceased father's last name had been Rizzo. Everyone called her mother Mirella. He'd heard the story that her husband, who worked in the estate stables, had died of an infection in his leg. After that, Mirella moved up from the village where they'd lived before his death and was allowed rooms in the rear of the *castello* with her little girl, Gemma.

One of the cooks who'd lived there, too, had had a child of the same age, named Bianca. Vincenzo couldn't remember when he and his cousin Dimi had started playing with them on the grounds of the estate. They were probably four and five years old.

Strict lines between social classes were drawn to prevent them from being together, but like all children, they found a way. He remembered his eighth birthday, when Gemma entered the courtyard where he and Dimi had been practicing archery with his new bow. She gave him a little lemon ricotta cheesecake her mother had baked just for him. He'd never tasted anything so good in his life.

From that day on, Gemma found ways to slip sweets to him from the kitchen. They'd go to their hiding place at the top of the tower and sit outside, straddling the crenellated wall while they ate his favorite *sfogliatelli*. When he looked down from that same wall now, he realized they could have fallen to their deaths at any time.

An hour later he went to bed, but he couldn't turn

off his thoughts. When he'd had to leave Europe in the dead of night, he hadn't been able to tell Gemma why and hadn't dared make contact with her. Days, weeks, months and finally years went by, but she'd always lingered in his memory.

To think that while he'd been in New York buying and selling businesses and building new companies over the last decade, she'd been in Florence working heaven knew how many hours, day in and day out, before ending up back at the *castello* as executive pastry chef. *Incredibile!*

CHAPTER THREE

GEMMA HAD BEEN in a state of disbelief since last night. A Signor Manolis, the business manager, had called to tell her she'd been hired to be the executive pastry chef at the Castello Supremo Hotel and Ristorante di Lombardi! She was to report to him at noon today.

Things like this just didn't happen, not to a new culinary graduate. But it was, and it meant she didn't have to leave Italy. By some miracle she was going back to where she'd known years of happiness...being friends and falling in love with Vincenzo before that dreadful moment when she'd learned of his disappearance.

Don't think about that terrible morning when the duca *destroyed your life and your mother's. That part of your life was over a long time ago. Let the memories go...you're the new pastry chef. And now it's possible you can find out what happened to Vincenzo.* One of her new bosses had to have information.

But a huge new problem beset her.

How was she going to tell her mother about this? Her dear mother, who was in England and knew nothing yet.

Gemma flew around the room in a panic. How

would her *mamma* react to this after all the many sacrifices she'd made for her daughter over the years?
Would it be like pouring acid on a wound? Or could
Gemma make her see that this might just be the way
to turn the ugliness around?

And what greater triumph than for Mirella's
daughter to arrive at the *castello* as executive pastry
chef? Gemma's mother had been hired by the old,
beloved *duca*, Vincenzo's grandfather. Now Mirella's daughter would be following in her footsteps.
Best of all, her mother wouldn't have to leave Italy
and could stay in Florence if she wanted to. These
thoughts and more filled her mind while she tried to
convince herself this could work.

After showering, she decided to wear her other
suit, consisting of a navy skirt and a short-sleeved
white jacket with navy piping and buttons. Though
she swept her wavy hair back with a clip when she
cooked, today she left it to hang down to her shoulders from the side part.

Being five foot seven, she mostly wore comfortable flats for cooking. But on this special occasion
she wanted to look her best and slipped on strappy
navy heels. Tiny pearl studs were the only jewelry
she wore besides her watch and her grandmother's
ring she would always wear in remembrance of her.

Gemma didn't need blusher. Excitement had filled
her cheeks with color. With a coating of frost-pink
lipstick and some lemon-scented lotion, she was ready
and walked out to her car without her feet touching
the ground.

After stopping at the same trattoria for breakfast,
she headed for the *castello*. Four days ago she'd been

upset that she couldn't apply for a position in France. But she hadn't known what was awaiting her at the former ducal residence in Milan.

Yesterday she'd worked alongside another applicant who was hoping to be chosen executive head chef. The five-star hotel he'd come from in Paris was renowned throughout Europe. To be stolen to work here meant he was the best of the best.

Gemma had taken French and English all the years she'd ever gone to school. Her mother had insisted on it, which had turned out to be advantageous for her. Some of her classes at the culinary school had been taught by various French experts, and she'd been thankful she didn't have to struggle with the language.

After they'd been introduced, she wouldn't say Monsieur Troudeau was rude. If anything he treated her as if she were invisible. No chitchat. Naturally he was shocked that such a young woman was vying for the pastry chef position. She'd ignored him and had concentrated on the pastries she'd planned to make.

The newly renovated kitchen with state-of-the-art equipment had been a dream. If only her mother could have worked under such unparalleled conditions…but that was in the past. Perhaps her mother could come to the *castello* and see the way it had been renovated. And instead of the ducal staff and family, Gemma would now be making pastry for the jet set, royals, celebrities and dignitaries of the world. She still couldn't believe it.

This time when she drove up to the front of the *castello*, she saw a black Maserati parked there. Maybe it belonged to the business owner with the strong accent who'd phoned her. Gemma got out of her car and hurried up the steps. When she entered the lobby of the hotel, she saw a fit, dark blond man, maybe six foot one and thirtyish, waiting for her behind the counter. His hazel eyes swept over her.

"You must be Signorina Bonucci. I'm Takis Manolis."

"How do you do?" She shook his hand. The signor was another good-looking man, dressed more formally in a suit and tie. This one had rugged features and probably needed to shave often. He spoke passable Italian and reminded her of some of the guys she'd met at school, possibly Turkish or Greek.

"I'm still trying to come down from the clouds since your phone call."

He flashed her a quick smile. "Congratulations."

Her eyes smarted. "I'm so happy I could burst."

"We're happy, too. Now that we've found you, we can get going on the preparations for the grand opening. If you'll come back to my office, we'll start the paperwork and sort out all the little details to make this a happy working experience for you."

Once again she found herself walking around the counter and followed him to one of the offices down the hallway. He kept his room tidy and asked her to sit down while he took his place behind the desk.

When they'd finished, he told her to report for work the day after tomorrow at nine in the morning. All staff would be assembled in the grand ballroom off the dining room for an orientation meeting to meet the new owners. Throughout the day there would be sessions to discuss policies, after which she would meet with the newly hired kitchen staff. "Do you have any questions?"

"Just one, but it doesn't have anything to do with the position. Would you be able to tell me how it is that the Gagliardi family no longer lives here? I once lived here with my mother, who cooked for the old *duca*. I find it impossible to believe that this magnificent monument, if you will, has been turned into a hotel after centuries of being the ducal seat of the region."

He studied her for a moment, but it gave her a strange feeling. "You'll have to speak to the only man who can answer that question for you."

At last there was someone who knew something. "Do you have a phone number where I can reach him?"

"I can do better than that. If you'll wait here, I'll send him in to you." He got up from the chair and left the room.

Her heart began to thud while she waited. Maybe this man would be able to tell her where she could find Vincenzo. Perhaps this man could tell her where he'd gone that night or where Dimi was. It seemed impossible for a family to just vanish.

What if he's not alive? That question had haunted her for years. *No, no. Don't think that way.* By now he was probably married to a princess and had children he adored.

Gemma couldn't bear to think that he might have found someone else. *Oh, Gemma. You're still the same lovesick fool from years ago.*

Vincenzo was on the phone with Annette when Takis walked in on him. "She's in my office waiting for you," his friend whispered before leaving him alone.

His pulse sped up. Gemma was only a door away.

"Vince? Didn't you hear me?" Annette asked him.

He sucked in his breath. "Yes," he said in English, "but someone just came in and it's important. I promise to call you by this evening, my time."

"I hope you mean that."

"Of course."

"We haven't been together for five weeks. I miss you terribly."

He just couldn't tell her the same thing back. "I have to go. Talk to you later."

He rang off and got to his feet, dressed in trousers and a polo shirt. To see Gemma again meant facing demons he'd tried to repress for years. Too many emotions collided at the same time—anxiety, excitement, curiosity, pain, guilt. Terrible guilt.

She'd been with him the night he'd been at his most vulnerable. The night after that, he'd been forced to flee before more tragedy could befall the family. The two of them had only been seventeen and eighteen, yet the memory of those intense feelings was as fresh to him right now as it had been ten years ago.

Since he'd returned to Italy, thoughts of Gemma had come back full force. At times he'd been so preoccupied, the guys were probably ready to give up on him. To think that after all this time and searching for her, she was right here. Bracing himself, he took the few steps necessary to reach Takis's office.

With the door ajar he could see a polished-looking woman in a blue-and-white suit with dark honey-blond hair falling to her shoulders. She stood near the desk with her head bowed, so he couldn't yet see her profile.

Vincenzo swallowed hard to realize Gemma was no longer the teenager with short hair he used to spot when she came bounding up the stone steps of the *castello* from school wearing her uniform. She'd grown into a curvaceous woman.

"Gemma." He said her name, but it came out gravelly.

A sharp intake of breath reverberated in the office. She wheeled around. Those unforgettable brilliant green eyes with the darker green rims fastened on him. A stillness seemed to surround her. She grabbed hold of the desk.

"Vincenzo—I—I think I must be hallucinating."

"I'm in the same condition." His gaze fell on the lips he'd kissed that unforgettable night. Their shape hadn't changed, nor the lovely mold of her facial features.

She appeared to have trouble catching her breath. "What's going on? I don't understand."

"Please sit down and I'll tell you."

He could see she was trembling. When she didn't do his bidding, he said, "I have a better idea. Let's go for a ride in my car. It's parked out front. We'll drive to the lake at the back of the estate, where no one will bother us. Maybe by the time we reach it, your shock will have worn off enough to talk to me."

Hectic color spilled into her cheeks. "Surely you're joking. After ten years of silence, you suddenly show up here this morning, honestly thinking I would go anywhere with you?"

He'd imagined anger if he ever had the chance to see her again. But he'd never expected the withering ice in her tone. Her delivery had debilitated him.

"Four days ago I applied for a position at this new hotel. Yesterday I was told I'd been hired, and now you walk in here big as life. I feel like I'm in the middle of a bizarre dream where you're back from the dead."

That described his exact state of mind. "You're not the only one feeling disoriented," he murmured. He felt as if he'd been thrown back in time, but they were no longer teenagers, and she was breathtaking in her anger.

"How long have you been in Milan?"

"Over the last six months I've made many trips here from New York."

"New York," she whispered. A crushed expression broke out on her face.

"When Dimi told me the *castello* had gone into receivership, two of my friends in New York and I decided to go into business with Dimi and turn it into a hotel. We couldn't let our family home be seized by the government or sold off to a foreign entity."

"It's yours by right, surely, unless that was a lie, too."

"It *was* mine by right...once. But that's a long story."

She shook her head. "I tried to imagine where you'd gone. I'd supposed you had friends somewhere in Europe, but it never occurred to me you would leave for the States." Gemma rubbed her hands against her hips in a gesture of abject desolation.

Vincenzo pushed ahead with the story he'd decided to use as cover. "I'd turned eighteen and decided it was time I made my mark and proved myself by making my own money. But my father would never have approved, so I had to leave without his knowledge."

"Or mine," she whispered so forlornly it shattered him.

"I couldn't do it any other way." He didn't dare tell her the real circumstances. She'd suffered enough. Vincenzo's guilt was so great, he was more convinced than ever that she'd been better off without him and still needed protection from the hideous truth.

"Are you trying to tell me that there wasn't even one moment in ten years when you could send me as much as a postcard to let me know you were alive?" Her voice was shaking, partly with rage, partly pain. He could hear it because pain echoed in his heart, too.

"I didn't know where to write to you, let alone call you. Dimi didn't know where you'd gone and looked endlessly for you. You'll never know how I've suffered over that."

He heard another sharp intake of breath. "Are you honestly trying to tell me that you looked for me?"

The depth of her pain was worse than he'd imagined. "Over the last ten years I've had private investigators searching for you. I've never stopped."

"I don't believe you." It came out like a hiss. "Has Dimi been in New York with you, too?"

"No. He lives in Milan with Zia Consolata."

Her face paled, and a hand went to her throat. A nerve throbbed at the base where he'd kissed her many times.

"I've heard all I need to hear."

In the next breath, she moved toward the door. Before he could comprehend, she flung it open and raced down the hall to the lobby. He'd never seen her in high heels before. She moved fast on those long gorgeous legs of hers.

Vincenzo started after her, noticing her hair swish and shimmer in the sunshine with every movement. He didn't catch up until she'd reached her car. Too many questions about her life were battering him at once. He wanted to make up to her for all the pain he'd put her through by disappearing without a word. Vincenzo couldn't let her get away from him. Not now.

"Where do you think you're going?"

She ignored him and opened the car door. He was aware of a lemon scent coming from her that assailed his senses. Right this minute her fragrance and femininity wrapped around him like they had done years ago, and his desire for her was palpable.

Once seated, she slammed the car door. Through the open window he saw her put the key in the ignition.

"We have to talk, Gemma!"

Her cheeks had turned scarlet with anger. "That's how I felt for days, weeks, months, even years until the need was burned out of me."

"You don't mean that," he ground out.

"Let me explain it this way. Remember our discussion about one of the films of the *Count of Monte Cristo*? If you don't, I do. Mercedes had waited years for Edmond Dantes, the man she loved. But when he suddenly appeared years later, he'd changed beyond recognition and she said goodbye to him.

"I related totally to her feelings then and now. I celebrate your return to life and all the billions of dollars you've made in New York, Vincenzo Gagliardi. I wish you well. Please tell the business manager that

I've changed my mind and won't be taking the job after all. *Arrivederci*, signor."

Wild with pain, Gemma backed away and flew down the road leading to the town below. Her eyes stung. By the time she reached the *pensione*, she realized she'd lashed out for all the years she'd been crushed by his silence.

And for his being so damned gorgeous it hurt to look at him. In ten years he'd grown into a stunning man. Standing six foot three with hard muscles and hair black as midnight, he was the personification of male beauty in her eyes.

She could hardly breathe when he'd walked into Signor Manolis's office. No wonder she hadn't been able to go on seeing Paolo. The memory of Vincenzo had always stood in the way. *He* was the reason she hadn't been able to find happiness with another man.

When they'd been together for the last time, he'd imprinted himself on her. She'd read about such things in books of fiction, but the love she'd felt for him had been real and life changing.

To think she'd suffered ten years before learning that he'd left Italy with the sole desire to earn money! Being the *duca* apparent wasn't enough. All the time they'd been growing up, he'd never once shown signs of greed in his nature. But it turned out he was just like his father!

The moment he'd reached legal age, he'd disappeared like a rabbit down a hole to add more assets to the massive family fortune. Apparently if you were a Gagliardi with a title, you could never have enough!

She couldn't credit it. And no one had known where he'd gone except Dimi.

Because of Gemma's involvement with the *duca*'s son, her mother had paid a huge price the night he'd taken off without telling his father. Shame on her for believing in something that had been a piece of fiction in her mind and heart. How many times had her mother tried to pound it in her head that she and Vincenzo would always be worlds apart?

She could hear her mother's voice. She and Vincenzo hadn't just been two ordinary teenagers indulging in a romantic fantasy. She was from the lower class, while he was an aristocrat who would one day become the Duca di Lombardi.

Any woman he married would have to be a princess, like his aunt and his mother. Day in and day out, her mother had cautioned her against her attachment to Vincenzo, but Gemma hadn't listened, so sure she was of his love.

After she reached the *pensione*, her troubled cry resounded in the car's interior. If she hadn't applied for the position at the *castello*, they would never have seen each other again in this lifetime.

You simply can't let what he's done destroy your life.

For a few minutes she struggled for composure so the *padrona di casa* wouldn't know anything was wrong. Then Gemma went inside to gather her things before driving back to Florence. Her cousin wouldn't have to know what had gone on. Gemma could simply tell her she was still looking for a position but that it would take some time.

While she packed her toiletries in the bathroom,

there was a knock on the door. Gemma told the *padrona* to come in.

"*Scusi*, signorina." She shut the door. "There's a gentleman outside from the *castello* wishing to speak to you in private."

Her heart knocked against her chest, but she kept packing and tried to feign nonchalance. "Who is it?"

"Signorina—" She ran over to her with excitement. "I would never have believed it, but it's the dashing young Duca di Lombardi himself, all grown up."

She trembled. "Surely you're mistaken." What else could she say?

"No, years ago the police looked for him and circulated pictures." Gemma remembered those policemen. "I would know him anywhere. He has the Gagliardi eyes."

She moaned. Those silvery eyes were legendary. Had he decided to use his title with the *padrona* to get what he wanted? Gemma hadn't thought Vincenzo would go so far as to follow her here, but like his father, he did whatever he wanted. Well, he couldn't force her to work at the restaurant!

Now that Gemma had shown up on his radar, it seemed he'd decided it was all right to fulfill the role destined for him from birth. Though she wanted to ask the *padrona* to tell Vincenzo she wasn't available, she couldn't do that. The older woman wasn't a servant, and Gemma didn't want her involved.

"Thank you for telling me. I'm leaving now and going back to Florence. I've left your money on the table. You've been very kind."

Gemma picked up her bag and walked outside to find Vincenzo lounging against the front of her car with his strong arms folded. The *padrona* smiled at him one last time before disappearing back through the doors.

Gemma put her bag in the rear seat. "Why did you follow me? I thought I made it clear that I can't accept the position of pastry chef. You're crazy if you're trying to expunge your guilt this way. Perhaps not guilt, exactly... A *duca* doesn't suffer that emotion like normal people, right? Yet he's known to give payment to someone like the cook's daughter for past services rendered. However, I can assure you that it's wasted on me."

A little nerve throbbed at the side of his compelling mouth, a mouth she'd kissed over and over before he'd told her she had to leave. "Is that what I'm doing?" he fired in a wintry voice.

"Yes! I'm quite sure you didn't offer the new executive chef a room at the *castello*, but Signor Manolis was told to offer me one."

The brief silence on his part upset her even more, because he didn't deny it.

"I knew it! The truth is, I don't deserve this job. The offer was too good to be true. I sensed there had to be a catch somewhere. I just didn't realize *you* had everything to do with it."

"Would it be so terrible of me to want to do something for you after the way I left without telling you? Let me make this up to you."

"I don't want anything from you, Vincenzo."

"If you're worried about the bedroom at the *castello*, I promise it won't be the back room behind the kitchen where you and your mother once lived."

"It's a moot point, but I wouldn't mind if it were."

"Nevertheless, all of that area was renovated along with the kitchen. The offer for you to stay at the *castello* will always stand."

"Why aren't you listening to me? I was shattered that you didn't say goodbye, that you didn't even let me know you were alive, but as for the rest, you owe me nothing!"

"That's not true."

"Think back to that night! Because you were in too much physical pain from that terrible fall from your horse, we didn't make love, even if we came close. Let's not forget I was as eager as you. Those moments happen to teenagers all the time! I had the hots for you, as they say in the US."

He grimaced. "Where did you learn that expression?"

"I picked up some American slang from the students at culinary school. So forget trying to fix what can't be fixed. I don't want to be compensated with a position of this magnitude or the extra perks that come with it. I understand there are two other applicants you can choose from."

"Three, but that's not the issue here."

She hadn't known that. "Then there's no problem."

Lines darkened his striking features. "You're wrong, Gemma. As for your expertise as a chef, the desserts made by you overwhelmed the committee. You have to know the decision to hire you was unanimous."

"I'll never really know, will I?"

His chest rose and fell visibly. "What do I have to do to convince you? Both Takis and Cesare are connoisseurs of fine food and wine. They recognize what will bring heads of state, kings, princes and world celebrities to the hotel over and over again. They chose you."

"Does it matter? I have interviews with two restaurateurs in Barcelona and London. If one of them hires me, I'll know I got the job for my cooking ability, nothing else."

She climbed behind the wheel. At least he didn't try to stop her.

"Where are you going?"

"Back to Florence."

"To the Bonucci Bakery? I saw the address on your application."

"Yes."

He stood there with his legs slightly apart, piercing her with those fabulous eyes. "You'll be driving in heavy traffic."

Since when had that become a concern? For the last ten years he hadn't known if she were dead or alive. He'd been flying from New York to Milan for the last six months on business. Her temper flared again.

"Vincenzo—I haven't been a teenager for years and I love to drive." She started the engine.

He moved closer. "Before you leave, tell me about your mother. How is she?"

Her bitter laugh shook him to the core. "She's alive and well, not that you'd care or be the least bit interested. Now I really have to go."

To her profound relief, he stepped back so she could drive away. Through the rearview mirror she saw his incredibly male physique standing there until she rounded the next corner.

The irony of running away from him after looking for him all these years wasn't lost on her. She drove back to Florence feeling as if she'd jumped off a precipice into the void.

CHAPTER FOUR

VINCENZO REACHED FOR his phone and left a message for the guys to say that he wouldn't be back at the *castello* until late. There were other calls from his assistant and his attorney in New York on his voice mail. None of them sounded urgent. He would deal with them later. But Annette's latest message demanded his attention. Earlier that morning he'd promised to call her back.

After putting on his sunglasses, he climbed in his Maserati and followed Gemma to Florence. The satellite navigation would lead him to the Bonucci Bakery. There was no way he would let her turn things around and disappear on him. He needed the chance to talk to her. The depth of her pain had caused him to reel. This was worse than anything he'd imagined if he'd ever seen her again.

While he was en route, he phoned Annette.

"Is it possible you've found some time for me?" she teased, but he heard her underlying impatience and didn't blame her.

"I'm sorry, but I've had business that has taken priority."

"Vince, you seem different. What's wrong?"

There was no way to explain to her what was going on inside him right now. But Annette deserved to hear how he felt even if it was going to hurt her. "You've asked me before if there was a special woman in my life. I've told you no and would never lie to you about that. But in my youth I fell in love with an Italian girl I haven't seen or heard from in ten years. Today I met up with her by accident."

He was still trying to recover.

After an ominous quiet, she said, "So what are you saying? That after all this time you find you're still in love and don't want me to come for the opening?"

He took a deep breath. "I'm saying that a big portion of my past caught up with me today. To be frank, I'm reeling." It wouldn't have been fair to lie to her.

"I sensed there was someone else all this time. She must have a powerful hold on you for those feelings to have lasted over a decade."

"Annette, I can't honestly tell you where this is headed."

What he did know was that seeing Gemma again had stirred up longings in him more intense than he could ever have imagined. To find out that Gemma wasn't married yet was a miracle. But her anger had been so intense, he needed to talk to her about it.

"Neither can I," Annette murmured. "Under the circumstances, I don't intend to wait for calls from you that might not come."

"I haven't meant to hurt you."

"I realize that, but on my part I always felt something was holding you back. If you ever figure it out and find yourself whole of heart, you know where to find me."

Even deeply upset, she had a graciousness and maturity he had to admire. "I'm sorry, Annette. Give me some time and I'll get back to you."

"I won't be holding my breath, Vince."

He heard the click.

Though Vincenzo hadn't wanted to cause her pain, his sense of relief that he didn't have to pretend with her had removed a burden. He'd told her the only truth he knew, since he needed time to deal with his emotions.

The reality of seeing Gemma again, the incredible coincidence that she'd applied for the pastry chef position, had knocked the foundations from under him.

At ten after six, he entered Florence at the height of evening traffic and found the Bonucci pastry shop. After searching everywhere for her old Fiat, he drove around the corner into an alley. Her blue car sat beside a stairway leading to the second floor of the bakery.

He found another spot along the crowded one-way street. Once he'd parked his car at the rear of the *pasteria* next door, he took the steps two at a time to the little porch outside her door. To think all these years since leaving the *castello* this place had been her home. How could he or Dimi have known?

He knocked twice.

Soon he heard, "*Chi e?*"

He was glad she didn't automatically open the door. Anyone could be out here. "It's Vincenzo. I would have phoned you I was coming, but I wasn't sure you would answer."

There was a long silence. "Go away!"

"I can't. Surely you can see that," he fought back. "I never expected any of this to happen. Even if you

refuse to come to work for us, how could you think
I would just let you drive away?"

"I'm not going to open my door. Go back to your
home, Vincenzo."

What home? He hadn't known that feeling in the
ten years since he'd last been with her. He broke out
in a cold sweat. So much damage had been done, he
didn't know if he could repair any of it, even if he
told her the real truth of everything.

"Would you deny your time to any other person
you knew well in the past who wanted to get reacquainted after a long period of separation? Since I've
come all this way and am starving, let's have dinner
at the *pasteria* next door. We'll order some wine and
reminisce over a time when life was wonderful for
both of us."

"That would be a mistake."

"You don't recommend the food? If anyone would
know whether it was good or not, you're the one."

"Be serious, Vincenzo," she snapped.

"I'm trying to be. You have no idea how isolated
I've felt all these years. Dimi and I are the only ones
left who can talk about that other life and relate. Our
fathers kept us under virtual lock and key, with body-
guards controlling everything we did. You better than
anyone know that they only allowed us to have a few
friends they picked.

"But all these years there's been a huge hole, and
you know why. Because that other life included you.
I need a few hours with you, Gemma." His voice
shook. "Will you grant me that much?"

He waited for her response. "You're not the person I thought you were, Vincenzo. Otherwise you

wouldn't have left without so much as a goodbye. I was never good enough for you, we both know that. We've led separate lives since your disappearance, and we were never the same people growing up."

His eyes closed tightly, but her pain kept her talking.

"You're from one world and I'm from another. A little while ago the reminder came from the *padrona*, who said the Duca di Lombardi was standing outside waiting to see me. There's no need for us to talk or be with each other again, Vincenzo."

She knew where to thrust through to the gut. Her mother had done a sensational job of indoctrinating her over the nonsense of ancient class distinctions he couldn't abide.

"If I swear on my mother's soul to leave you strictly alone, will you accept the position at the *castello* to see us through the first three months? Takis and Cesare will be the ones working with you. I'll stay out of your way unless there's a professional reason why I have to talk to you about something."

Was she even listening?

"You can put me on probation, Gemma. If I make one mistake, you can leave immediately, no questions asked. If at the end of the three months you still want to leave, you'll receive impeccable recommendations and be given a generous severance package of your choosing."

"Why would you enter into an arrangement like that when you know how I feel?"

"Because your expertise as a pastry chef is unparalleled. My partners will be bitterly disappointed to learn that you've refused the position because you can't forgive me for my past sins."

"It's not a matter of forgiveness. The trust is gone."

Vincenzo couldn't take this much longer. "*They* trust me. You have to understand that I asked them to go into business with me. But for me they wouldn't be here. Not only my integrity, but their financial lives and reputations are on the line. Like me, they want our business venture to work."

"As you told me earlier, you have three other applicants eager to work there."

"My friends don't want anyone else and are convinced that with everything we've put in place including your cooking, we'll succeed beyond our wildest dreams. I *know* we will, because I grew up on your mother's delicacies that you've perfected. You have no equal, Gemma."

"Please leave."

"I only have one more thing to say. You don't have to make a decision this very minute. I'm on my way back to Milan." *I've got to stop and see Dimi.* He wasn't going to believe Gemma had been found.

"Gemma? If you don't show up for your first orientation meeting with rest of the staff the day after tomorrow, then I'll tell my partners you found you couldn't accept the position after all because of a family emergency at the bakery. Naturally we'll choose one of the other pastry chef finalists."

She still said nothing.

His pain had reached its zenith. "*Arrivederci, tesoro.*"

Gemma gasped. The night in his bedroom when they'd been wrapped in each other's arms, he'd called her his treasure. While her world spun in reaction to that endearment, she watched out the window. His car traveled down the street until she couldn't see him anymore.

Surely to accept his offer would mean that she had no self-control, that all he had to do was summon her in his inimitable, seductive way and she'd come running.

What else could she expect when Vincenzo's immoral father and uncle had been his role models? He might not think he could ever behave as they'd done, but the precedent had been set for decades. Once he married a princess and had children, the need for distraction would come.

With business enterprises on either side of the Atlantic, he'd have ample opportunities to be with women his wife wouldn't know about. Or would pretend not to know about. Who better than the adoring daughter of the former cook to fill the position as one of his mistresses and provide him amusement during secret getaways when he was in Italy?

Gemma, unmarried and childless, wouldn't have a life while she waited for those moments of rapture with him. Little by little his need for her would grow more infrequent while she went on getting older and more unfulfilled. Over the centuries, women of the lower class had done as much in order to be with the titled men they'd loved, but Gemma refused to be one of them!

She'd been afraid he'd break her down with words like this. Somehow he was succeeding despite her determination not to listen or be moved. Tears dripped from her eyes while she called Filippa, who'd just come out of a bad relationship.

Her friend knew Gemma's history. When she heard Vincenzo was back in Gemma's life, she cried out in shock. For the next hour Gemma told her everything.

Before they hung up, Filippa asked her one salient question. "Did he ever do anything in his past that caused you not to trust him until the day when you learned he had disappeared?"

"No. But we're grown up now, and he's the *duca*. I can't see our lives together in any way, shape or form."

"From what you've told me, he hasn't asked for more than a three-month probationary period to help him get their restaurant off the ground. He wants you to have this position because you were the top applicant. Naturally he wants to make it up to you for leaving without an explanation."

"I know."

"Remember that he said he needed to make money and couldn't let his father find out his plans. That sounds like a strong reason for what he did. And don't forget he said he looked for you over all these years. So what more can he do to make you feel any better? You *did* sign on with them in good faith, and they did, too."

Gemma sniffed. Put that way, there was no argument. "You're right."

"If I were you, I'd agree to his offer. He promised to leave you alone away from work, and he would be a fool if he reneges. Just think, Gemma—the opportunity to be the head pastry chef there will give you entrée anywhere in the world when you leave. With a five-star recommendation, you'll have carte blanche with whichever wonderful restaurant in France you'd like and you could realize your dream."

Filippa made it sound possible, even easy. But she'd never met Vincenzo Gagliardi and had no comprehension of the man Gemma had always loved. Every day of those three months she worked at the *castello*, she'd be in agony thinking about him, desiring him. Was he on the premises, or was he in New York? How soon would the media reveal breaking news about the fiercely handsome, dashing Duca di Lombardi coming back home? Which gorgeous princess would be the one to catch his eye and become his bride and the mother of his children?

"Gemma? Are you still there?"

She blinked away the moisture. "Yes, of course. I was deep in thought. Sorry."

"So what are you going to do?"

"I'm not sure, but I love you for listening to me and helping me sort through my pain."

"You've done the same thing for me too many times to count. I've got to go right now. Let me know what you finally decide."

"I will. Ciao, Filippa."

"Ciao, *amica*."

While Gemma fixed herself an omelet, she reran their conversation over in her mind. By the time she went to bed, her pragmatic side had taken over. She needed a job and had been offered one that would make her the envy of everyone at her school. There was no way she could turn down his offer.

When she gave her mother the news, she'd tell her it was only for a three-month period. But she'd wait to tell her *mamma* anything until Mirella got back from her vacation. By then Gemma would have lined up another job so that when the three months were up, they'd leave Lombardi and the *castello* behind.

With a top recommendation, she would be set up to find a great restaurant in the South of France that would hire her. In time she could accrue enough savings to put down roots.

Gemma had dreamed of buying a little villa in Vence or Grasse with a garden and some fruit trees overlooking the Mediterranean. She'd won an award for her jam. Since her mother would be living with her, maybe they'd make their own and sell it locally. Anything could happen. Filippa had made her see that.

For now she would have to trust Vincenzo to keep their bargain. As she'd told her friend, she'd trusted Vincenzo in the past. It would be her own fault if she couldn't remain strong and stay away from him.

Grateful for her friend's advice, she woke up early the next morning and got busy house cleaning. When her mother and aunt returned from England, they'd find the place spotless. At four that afternoon, she left with her large suitcase and went down the steps to her car parked in the alley. It was best her cousin didn't know where she was going until Gemma had told her mother everything first.

When she reached Sopri, she called on the *padrona di casa* and told her she would like to stay at the *pensione* for a three-month period because she'd be working at the new hotel. Would that be possible?

The older woman couldn't have been more delighted and they settled on a good price. "You'll be working for the *duca*. Any arrangement you want is fine." On that note she let Gemma into the room she'd had before with a huge smile. Such was Vincenzo's effect on every female, young or old.

Gemma got settled in and pulled out her laptop. She needed to send emails to London and Barcelona and thank them for setting up appointments with her. In her note she told them she was sorry but she'd found another position. If by any chance it didn't work out at the *castello*, she wondered if they would allow her to reapply?

Once that was done, she got ready for bed and lay back against the pillows. Tomorrow morning she'd be meeting with Signor Donati at nine for the orientation meeting. The newly hired kitchen staff would also be present. Being part of a hotel, the restaurant would serve meals throughout the day and evening as well as provide room service. Such organization required a genius at the head.

Vincenzo.

Because he was the one who'd masterminded everything, he would always have input. She expected that. Naturally they'd see each other coming and going, much the same as they'd done ten years earlier. But this time everything would be different. In order to survive, she was forced to put on her armor and leave the sweet innocence of their youthful love in the past.

After confiding in Dimi the evening before, Vincenzo had worked through the night on his personal business affairs here in Italy. Establishing Nistri Technologies in the south of the country consumed a lot of his spare time, but that was good. He existed on coffee, trying not to think about what would happen if Gemma didn't show up today. He hadn't told the guys anything, not wanting to alarm them.

His cousin didn't have great hopes where Gemma was concerned. She was an unknown entity at this point. Vincenzo didn't like hearing Dimi's opinion but appreciated that his was the voice of reason.

After a shower and shave, he put on a business suit and tie before leaving his tower room to go downstairs. His watch said it was ten to nine, and already the ballroom appeared full. But as he looked around, his worst nightmare was confirmed, because Gemma was nowhere in sight.

His fear that she'd left Florence and he'd never see her again came close to paralyzing him, but for the guys' sake, he had to pull himself together. He'd wanted to hire security to keep an eye on her but had resisted the impulse. That's what his father had done to him and Dimi. He knew Gemma had already accused him in her heart of being like his father. He didn't dare make that mistake.

At their first break in the morning schedule, Vincenzo would take his partners aside and give them the bad news. While they ran the next segment without him, he would have to go to his office and contact their other applicants. If none of them were available, there was more work to do.

A blackness had descended on Vincenzo as he joined Takis in front of their awaiting audience. He was on the verge of asking him about Cesare when the Sicilian entered through the tall double doors.

Gemma followed him in. At the first sight of her, Vincenzo's heart kicked him in the ribs so hard he almost moaned aloud. Somehow she'd managed to put aside her hurt and anger enough to accept his proposition.

She'd come dressed in a fabulous peach-colored suit. It was a miracle he had any breath left. He couldn't take his eyes off her as she found a chair on the end of a row halfway toward the front. Vincenzo was still in a state of shock when Takis stood up with the microphone in hand.

"Welcome, everyone! Take a look around. The success of the new Castello Supremo Hotel and Ristorante di Lombardi is in your hands. By the end of the day it's our hope you'll feel like family. It's the only way our enterprise will work."

Vincenzo had hoped everyone they'd hired would feel like family. After all the work he and his partners had done over the last six months, he couldn't help but be proud of what they'd accomplished so far.

He was happy that he'd asked the guys to employ as many local staff as possible, especially those who hadn't been able to find work lately. It was a way to give back to the community that had been harmed because his father and uncle had been such bad people.

For a long time he'd been worried that he'd involved his friends in a project that could have professional as well as personal repercussions if things didn't go well. But Gemma's appearance a minute go went a long way to help calm some of those fears. With both of them together again in the same room, he felt an odd sense of rightness.

"At your interviews, you were given a small history of the *castello*. For as long as you work here, guests will ask you repeatedly about this iconic hundred-years-old structure. As you've learned, it was the home of the first Duca di Lombardi of the house of Gagliardi in the eighteen hundreds.

"Today I'm honored to introduce one of the owners and chief operating officer for the estate, security and publicity, Vincenzo Nistri Gagliardi, seated on my right."

A collective sound of surprise was followed by resounding applause that filled the room. With the media calling for information at this point, Vincenzo had given Takis permission to offer public disclosure of their three-owner enterprise. He'd felt it was time he embraced his name again. But there'd be no mention of the family title.

"I'm Takis Manolis, one of the owners and general manager of the hotel. On my left is Cesare Donati, the other owner and general manager for the restaurant." More clapping ensued.

Takis finished talking and handed Vincenzo the mic.

Vincenzo only intended to say a few words that would put the floating rumors to rest. "Some of you may know this was my home for the first eighteen years of my life. Though I've spent the last ten years in New York City, my roots are here."

The girl who made it my own private heaven is seated among you.

"My business partners and I hope this will become a desired destination for locals and tourists from around the globe. If we all work together, I know it will be a great success. Thank you."

This time everyone got to their feet and kept clapping. He handed the mic to Cesare and sat down.

His friend took over the reins. When the noise subsided, he introduced their head chef, Monsieur Maurice Troudeau. Then he turned to Gemma.

"In the words of Schiaparelli, 'a good cook is like a sorceress who dispenses happiness.' That would describe the Italian desserts of our executive pastry chef, Gemma Bonucci Rizzo. Please stand, signorina."

There was more applause.

Vincenzo's pride in her accomplishments brought a lump to his throat. At the same time he couldn't stop his eyes from fastening on the lines of her beautiful figure.

Cesare continued to introduce the entire kitchen staff that also included the sous chefs, dishwashers, and front of house staff. Takis followed by introducing the front desk group, the head of housekeeping and the laundry staff. Then it was Vincenzo's turn once more to present the estate manager and gardeners. The security men made their own presentation.

After a ten-minute break, his partners met with the employees under them to get down to specifics on the job, including the hours they would work. That left Vincenzo to circulate.

He visited Takis's group first and added a few words. Then he walked to the kitchen, where Cesare laid out the hours for each shift and their duties, which included room service and the dining room. Vincenzo refused to look at Gemma. After saying a few more words of greeting, he made certain he stayed on the far side of the room away from her.

Gemma and Maurice had been asked to make out a day's worth of sample menus for the three meals they'd serve the day of the grand opening. Cesare looked them over before passing them to Vincenzo for his opinion. Since he didn't want to give Gemma any fuel to leave and never come back, he took the menus and walked to his office.

After sitting at his desk for a few minutes, he realized that having to distance himself from her was going to be the hardest thing he would ever have to do in his life. The key was to focus on work.

He spent the next few minutes studying her dessert choices, including the rolls, breads, preserves and jams she'd suggested to accompany Maurice's entrées and specialty dishes. They were both masters at what they did. He put his seal of approval on them.

But thoughts of Gemma made it impossible for him to stand his own company any longer. He walked to Cesare's office to give him the menus. His friend wasn't around. Vincenzo left them on his desk and went in search of Takis, who was still in the ballroom directing some of the newly hired staff to put the chairs away.

He waved. "*Ehi*, Vincenzo—all in all, I think it went well."

"I agree." But it would have been a disaster if Gemma hadn't shown up.

"Want to have drinks on the east patio later?"

"Sounds good, but I'll see. I have to run an errand, but I should be back soon."

Vincenzo hurried out of the *castello* to his car, too restless to stay put. After getting behind the wheel, he took off and drove aimlessly. He had a hunch Gemma had spent last night at the same *pensione* as before. If he returned by way of Sopri later, he assumed he'd see her car parked in front. But much as he wanted to find out where she was staying, he didn't dare.

Instead he ended up in the little village of Cisliano, only three miles from Sopri. He passed in front of the Rho Bistro. The owners had had the unique idea of waiting for all the customers to arrive. Then they started cooking the same menu for everyone and served it at one time.

Vincenzo had eaten there several times in his youth after a bike ride with Dimi, always being followed by a guard his father had hired. On his eighteenth birthday, he and Dimi had slipped away from their tutor and the guard. They'd arranged to meet Gemma and Bianca here.

He remembered that Friday as if it had been yesterday. Bianca's mother had taken pity on him and his cousin. She'd dropped the girls off and come back for them two hours later without telling Gemma's mother, who would have been upset.

The memory of that red-letter day had taken hold of him. Wanting to relive it, he decided to go in, but parking was difficult. He ended up driving around the corner to find a spot. For the moment all he cared about was soaking up those moments when he knew they'd been crazy in love with each other.

As usual, he discovered the noisy, unpretentious place was filled with summer customers at the dinner hour. There was one empty table in the corner partially separate from the others, probably available for any overflow. He grabbed it and was served coffee while everyone waited to be served.

CHAPTER FIVE

AFTER HER LAST meeting for the day, Gemma left the *castello* experiencing so many emotions, she didn't know where to go with all her feelings. Cesare's comments about her in front of the whole assembly had been very touching. She'd enjoyed the various sessions and had gotten on well with Maurice. But overriding everything was the realization that Vincenzo was back in Lombardi.

Along with his partners, they'd turned the *castello* into a hotel and restaurant that would definitely be the envy of other resorts in Italy. She'd felt the camaraderie among the people hired and had heard their praise for the new owners. The favorable whispers about Vincenzo would have pleased him.

Part of her had wanted to go to his office and thank him for this opportunity, but it was too difficult for her to be in such close proximity to him. She feared she wouldn't be able to fight her attraction to him. But the other part of her would always struggle, because he hadn't felt she was good enough to confide in before he'd disappeared. He'd created a deep wound that would never heal.

Where was the Vincenzo she would have done

anything for? On his eighteenth birthday, she'd dared to eat a meal with him at a restaurant outside the *castello*, even knowing they could both get into terrible trouble.

Caught up in the memory, she drove to Cisliano and found a parking place at the end of the street near the Rho Bistro. She and Bianca had spent two divine hours here with Vincenzo and Dimi. The need to recapture that moment took her inside, but the place was packed. As she looked around, her gaze suddenly collided with a pair of silver eyes staring at her between black lashes.

Vincenzo—her heart knocked against her ribs. He was here?

She watched as he got to his feet and walked over to her. "It appears you and I had the same idea this evening. As you can see, the whole world is here. You're welcome to join me at my table. I think I have the only free one left."

Gemma couldn't believe this had happened, but to turn him down would be churlish at this point.

"Thank you. I have to admit I'm starving."

No sooner had he held a chair for her to sit down than the waiters started bringing the food. The menu included antipasto, risotto, sautéed mushrooms, roasted polenta and potatoes, with a dessert of *limoncello* and iced cookies.

After a few bites she said, "I had no idea you were here."

"That works both ways." He sipped his coffee. "Seeing you again has made me nostalgic for my happy past, and I found myself driving here. The meal we enjoyed on my birthday will always stand out in my mind."

"Truthfully, I'll never forget it, either," she confessed. "On the way back to my flat, I decided to drive by and see if this place still existed. We were fed so much food, I didn't think I would ever eat again."

"You're not the only one."

"I was frightened someone from the *castello* would find out and word would get back to my mother. She would have grounded me forever."

"Three weeks after my birthday, I was in New York, ending our one and only over-the-*castello*-wall experience."

Over the wall was right! But Gemma didn't want to think about the past and changed the subject.

"After the last meeting in the kitchen, Cesare told us to go home and get a good sleep before we report in the morning ready to dig in. I didn't expect to see you here, but since we have bumped into each other, I'd like to thank you for giving me the opportunity to be the pastry chef. It *is* the chance of a lifetime."

"If anyone should be doing the thanking, it's me," he came back unexpectedly. "When I saw you walk into the ballroom this morning, I was able to breathe again. Later in my office I started looking over the menus. You and Maurice stimulate the brilliance in each other. There's no doubt in my mind the food at the Castello Supremo Ristorante will bring the world to our door."

"Coming from you, that's a great compliment." But Gemma wished he'd stop being so...so nice and charming the way he'd been years ago, the way he'd been today during the orientation meeting.

He kept talking. "Cesare is the true expert. The light in his eyes after he'd studied the menus and handed them to me told me all I needed to know about how excited he is about our new chefs." He drank more coffee.

"That's very gratifying to hear."

He flashed her a penetrating glance. "I can't believe you aren't married."

She drank her *limoncello* too quickly and started coughing. Had he been hoping she'd found a man? Would it make him feel less guilty for disappearing from her life? Why not turn things around on him?

"What about you, Vincenzo? You've been in New York all this time. I don't see a ring on your finger."

His mouth tautened. "I've been too busy conducting business to think about getting married."

No woman could resist him, so he couldn't have suffered in that department. But there probably weren't that many available princesses on the East Coast of the US to consider marrying. For that, he'd have to return to Europe. No doubt there'd been a short list compiled years ago for Vincenzo to consider.

She cleared her throat. "Labor-intensive work *does* have a way of interfering. Being an apprentice at the school hasn't allowed me the time to consider marriage. They require nine to ten years from you. That doesn't give you a spare moment to breathe." Except for that one month with Paolo, which was a mistake.

"Understood. As long as we're together, would you be willing to answer a question for me? Your last name is Rizzo, yet you used Bonucci on your application. Why?"

They were wading into dangerous waters now. "That's a long story."

"Is there some secret?"

Her eyes closed tightly. If he only knew.

"Bonucci is mother's maiden name. When we moved to the apartment above my aunt's bakery, Mamma told me to put Bonucci on my application. That way when I attended pastry school, it would be an easy identification with her family's bakery."

"Mirella was an intelligent woman and was always very kind to me and Dimi."

Just hearing him say her mother's name made her eyes smart. She nodded. "People love her. I love her terribly."

"Gemma," he murmured. "Don't you know I've missed that old life more than you can imagine? I know she's your whole world and you are hers. Interesting that after you left the *castello*, no one knew you as Gemma Rizzo. That's why neither Dimi nor I could find you."

Oh, no. She clenched her fists beneath the table. "Mamma would have done or said anything she could to—" Gemma stumbled "—to increase my chance to succeed."

She knew by the flicker in his eyes that he'd caught her correction. Vincenzo was a shrewd, brilliant businessman, and she was afraid he wouldn't let it go. "Your *mamma* got her wish. My colleagues have been praising your expertise." Heat crept into her cheeks again, but this time anger wasn't the culprit.

"That's very nice to hear. Now I've got to go so I'll be fresh for tomorrow."

"Gemma," he whispered. "What aren't you telling me?"

The tone in his voice reminded her of the old Vincenzo. Slowly, steadily, he was breaking her down. His magic was getting to her. *Damn, damn, damn.* Her heart pounded so hard, she was certain he could hear it. "I don't know what you mean."

"You forget I've known you since you were four years old. When you're nervous or afraid, your voice falters. You did it just now. You said that your mother would have done or said anything to...to what, Gemma? You left out something of vital importance. What was it?"

She felt sick inside. "You're wrong."

"Now your cheeks are red. They always fill with color when you're not telling the truth." He wouldn't stop until he'd wrung it out of her.

Vincenzo, Vincenzo. "Mamma said I had to say my last name was Bonucci in order to...protect me."

His handsome face darkened with forbidding lines. "From whom?"

"I—it was a long time ago and doesn't matter."

He let out an oath, and his brows formed a black bar above his eyes. "Did you get into trouble that night after you left my room? I still had to stay in bed the next day, so I didn't see you."

Gemma was thrown by the haunted sound in his voice. "No," she answered honestly.

"Why don't I believe you?"

"Vincenzo, I promise. After looking out the door that night, I snuck down the back staircase when I knew a guard wouldn't be there. No one saw me."

"Do you swear before God?" A vein stood out in his neck.

She sensed an unfathomable depth of anxiety here. It wasn't something he could hide. "Why have you asked me that?"

His body tensed. "Because if I thought my father had been waiting in the hall and did anything to you..."

"No one saw me." It was her turn to shudder at the degree of his concern. "I swear, nothing happened to me, Vincenzo."

"Keep talking to me, Gemma. There's still something else you haven't told me."

She stirred restlessly. Now was her chance to reveal every single cruel thing his father had done to her and her mother. But looking into his eyes and seeing the pain, she found she couldn't.

"Did you get questioned after my father found out I'd gone missing?" he demanded.

Give him some of the truth so he'll be satisfied.

"He and the police commissioner interrogated everyone at the *castello*, one at a time. No one knew anything about your disappearance. At that point they looked elsewhere for answers."

"Grazie a Dio."

She heard the tremendous relief in his voice, but by the way he was staring at her, she could tell he was far from finished with her, and she started to be afraid.

"When were you let go at the *castello*?"

Her pulse raced. "Does it matter? It's all in the past."

He shook his dark head. "Did it happen after my *nonno* died?"

"Yes," she said quietly, because with that question Gemma realized he really didn't know anything that had happened. Neither did Dimi, otherwise his cousin would have told him.

His sharp intake of breath was alarming. "You're lying to me again."

She jumped up from the chair. "I can't do this anymore. Thank you for letting me eat with you. Now I have to leave."

He looked up at her. "Where are you going?"

"Back to the *pensione*."

"If you leave now, you'll never know the true reason behind my sudden disappearance and why it had to be carried out in complete secrecy."

Stunned by what he'd just said, Gemma clung to the back of the chair. *The true reason?*

"On the strength of the years you and I spent together as children and teenagers who fell in love, isn't learning the whole truth worth something to you?"

"I thought you said you left to make your own fortune and name."

"That was a by-product of the real reason I left, but I didn't tell you the truth in order to spare you more grief. I can see now that I've been wrong to do that."

Along with everything he was saying, his confession that he'd been in love with her a long time ago was almost too much to bear. Gemma couldn't talk, couldn't think.

"I don't ever remember you running out of words before, so I'm following you home." He put some bills on the table. "We need privacy because we're not finished talking, but we can't do it here. People are watching."

"You made a promise."

"I would have kept it, but you've just told me another lie. If you don't want to work at the *castello* then I'll have to live with it, but I need the truth from you first. Let's go."

With her heart in her mouth, Gemma left the restaurant and walked to the end of the street to reach her car. She started the engine and pulled into traffic. Soon she was headed for Sopri.

Through the rearview mirror she could see the Maserati following closely behind. Adrenaline gushed through her veins. Finally she would know what had happened all those years ago. It didn't take long to reach the *pensione*. Vincenzo pulled up behind her and parked his car.

Without looking at him, she went inside, leaving the door open. He followed, closing it behind him.

"Come in and sit down. Take your pick of one of the chairs or the love seat."

Vincenzo did neither. First he looked around at the small, well-furnished flat. From the living room he could see part of the bedroom. Then he walked into the kitchen, where she was clinging to the counter.

This evening, the fear that he was losing his grip on Gemma had made him realize he had to tell her the painful truth about his disappearance if he ever hoped to have a chance of keeping her in his life. All the guilt and the shame would have to come out. He'd wanted to protect her, but it was too late for that now.

But first he needed to hear what had happened to her after he'd left. He sucked in his breath. "The truth,

Gemma. All of it! How soon after I disappeared did you and your mother leave the *castello*?"

She was trembling. "The second your father learned you were missing, he came with the chief of police and guards to our rooms at six that morning, demanding to know where you were. I told him I knew nothing. They searched our rooms before the police chief said he believed me.

"Your father told my mother to get out and take her baggage with her—meaning me, of course. Your father's outrage was frightening. The idea that his son, who would one day become the Duca di Lombardi, was enjoying life below the stairs with one of the cooks' daughters put him into a frenzy.

"He vowed to make certain she never got a job anywhere else. He threw Bianca and her mother out that same morning before he left with the police to start searching the countryside for you. That's why Mamma made me use the Bonucci name, so he couldn't find us."

Vincenzo's pain bordered on fury. He fought to stay in control. "What he did was inhuman. You should never have been forced to live through such a nightmare, and all because of me. I can never hope to make this up to you."

"It's over, and he was a sick man."

His jaw hardened. "More than sick. You don't know what a frenzy is until you've seen him raging drunk. My uncle was the same. Dimi had to get away, too."

She swallowed hard. "You said he lives in Milan with his mother."

He nodded. "They left the same day as you and

your mother did, while my father was out with the police hunting for me."

"When I first met your aunt Consolata, she was in a wheelchair. I always worried about her."

"I know you did. She always spoke of you with fondness, but she isn't well and has lost her memory."

"That's so sad."

This was the girl he'd remembered and dreamed about. She'd always had a sweetness and kindness that made her stand out from any woman he'd ever known.

"Did you ever hear how she ended up in her wheelchair?"

"Mamma told me she had a disease."

"No, Gemma," he ground out. "That was a story the family made up to cover the truth. My father and my uncle Alonzo were the ones with the disease."

"What do you mean?"

"They are alcoholics. Alonzo drove Dimi's mother home from a party when he was drunk out of his mind. She begged for someone else to drive her, but he became enraged and dragged her to the car. En route home, there was a terrible crash. The man in the other car was killed and Dimi's mother was paralyzed from the waist down, unable to walk again. But as usual, my father had it hushed up to protect the family honor."

Tears splashed down her cheeks.

"Just know that since my uncle has been imprisoned, Dimi and my aunt have been able to live in peace. But there's a lot more you need to hear in order for you to understand my sudden disappearance."

"A lot more?"

His fear for what his father might have done to her

triggered other thoughts. "The night we almost made love, you thought I'd been recovering from a fall after I'd been out horseback riding."

She nodded. "That's what they had been gossiping about down in the kitchen. I snuck upstairs that night to see how bad your injuries were."

"My bruises and welts weren't because of an accident, Gemma."

A cry escaped her lips. She looked ill. "Your *father* was responsible?"

"*Si.* He beat me almost to a pulp." Gemma winced. "But he did worse to my *mamma*, and she died because of it."

"Oh, Vincenzo—no—" Hot tears spurted from her eyes. "Why would he do that? She was a wonderful person."

"My parents' marriage was a political arrangement with a lot of money and land entailed. But my grandfather Count Nistri, the one who lived in Padua, didn't trust his new son-in-law. Even back then my father had a reputation for drinking and gambling. But he came from a family of great wealth and was a business wizard.

"To make certain his daughter, Arianna, my mother, always had security, he'd put a fortune in a Swiss bank account for her alone."

"He sounds like a loving man and father."

"He was, but my father resented me having any association with him. Still, he couldn't stop me from visiting him from time to time. My grandfather had the foresight and the means to help me get away when the time came."

"How did he do it?"

"Through a secret source, he learned my father had been badgering my mother for her money. At that point he gave her the information to access it and passports for both of us so we could escape."

Another gasp flew out of her.

"During the last year before she died, my father started hitting her when he couldn't get at her money. She couldn't withstand all those beatings." His eyes stung with tears. "Do you have any idea what I went through, hearing her cries while I was held back by the guards so I couldn't help her?"

Gemma covered her mouth in horror.

"I was helpless. He was the acting *duca*. He was the law. No one questioned him or his authority. If I'd sent for the police, they wouldn't have stopped him. Mamma needed me, but I failed her as her son."

"Of course you didn't!" Gemma cried. "Don't say that! Don't even think it!"

"For a long time she'd begged me to take the money and escape because she feared for my life. That's when I started to plan my disappearance, but I would never have left her behind. As far as escaping, I had to be an adult and couldn't go anywhere until I was of age.

"My uncle had no reason to stop his brother, since he was in worse trouble financially and was fighting to stay out of prison. To escape my father, I had to get as far away from Italy as possible. The US suited my plan perfectly."

She shook her head. "What plan?"

"The one Dimi and I devised a year before I left."

"A whole year, and you never once told me?" Her voice shook with pain.

"I didn't dare until I knew it was safe for you. But when that time came, you were nowhere to be found in Italy. Dimi hunted endlessly for you, too. When I escaped, our family had been unraveling at the speed of sound, Gemma, but until I turned eighteen and Mamma passed away, I couldn't do anything about it. If my father had gotten wind of anything, that would have been the end of me.

"Worse, if he'd found out that you knew where I'd gone, there's no telling what price you might have had to pay. As it was, your mother paid dearly for my disappearance. Thank heaven you got away without him beating you, too."

"This is a horror story."

"After Mamma's funeral, my father followed me to my room. He'd been drinking heavily. This time he beat me with his horse whip after I'd gone to bed."

At this point Gemma was quietly sobbing.

"He thought he could force the truth from me and get his hands on Mamma's fortune. As you know, he was a tall, powerful man. He would have succeeded in killing me if he hadn't been so drunk.

"Somehow I held him off. The next night was when you came up to my room looking for me. Your loving comfort and kisses held me together. But I was afraid my father would be back. That's why I couldn't let you stay the whole night with me. I was afraid if he found us, I wouldn't have the strength to protect you."

She'd buried her face in her hands. "I understand now."

"I'll always be in hell because I couldn't protect my mother."

She lifted her head. "Thank heaven you got out of

there alive. I remember the menacing look in your father's eyes. No wonder you were running for your life."

"The night after we were together, I made my get-away with Dimi's help. But leaving you without telling you anything was the hardest thing I'd ever had to do in my life. My cousin had to take the brunt of everything, and I asked him keep me informed about you. He was frantic because he didn't know where to look for you."

"I was so hurt and angry at you, I didn't even try to say goodbye to him. I'm so sorry now. He didn't have any way of knowing where we'd gone."

Without conscious thought Vincenzo wrapped her in his arms, and they clung while she sobbed. He wept in silence with her. After her tears subsided, she said, "Tell me what happened the night you left. I want to hear everything from the moment you left your room that night."

CHAPTER SIX

A MIRACLE HAD HAPPENED, because Gemma wanted to keep talking. Vincenzo kissed her hair and forehead.

"Let's go in the other room, where we can be comfortable." He walked her trembling body to the love seat, where she sat down, then he pulled the chair closer to be face-to-face with her.

"After I got up and dressed, I snuck to Dimi's tower room at two in the morning. We hugged and then I stole down the back staircase and through the old passage no longer used to reach the outside."

"I remember it."

"Knowing the guard wouldn't be able to see me yet, I raced through the gardens to reach the forest on the estate property without problem. The family cemetery plot was a good spot to rest. Then I ran past the lake and stables to the farthest edge of the property and hid up high in a tree until another guard had passed around the perimeter and disappeared."

"The dog didn't give you away?"

"It wasn't with him. That was another miracle. I stayed free of detection for twenty more minutes before climbing the fence. You should have seen me. I ran like hell down the hillside."

A little laugh escaped. "I can just see you!"

"My destination was a farm, where I waited behind a truck for the sun to come up."

"That must have been so scary."

"Not as scary as worrying that I'd be spotted before I jumped the perimeter fence. When I saw more activity on the road, I started walking to the village."

"Did anyone recognize you?"

"I put on a baseball cap and sunglasses."

She smiled. "I would have loved to see that."

"It did the trick. A half hour's walk and I reached the bus stop that took me into central Milan, where I got off near the main train station. After buying a one-way ticket to Geneva, I boarded a second-class car and found a group of German backpackers to sit by."

"Naturally you struck up a conversation with them. I know your royal tutors taught you four different languages, including German."

"My education came in handy during that four-hour train ride to Switzerland."

"Weren't you worried someone would recognize you?"

"I was lucky and made it to Geneva without problem."

"Thank heaven."

"Around three in the afternoon, the train arrived in Geneva. I said goodbye to the other backpackers and took a taxi to the Credit Suisse bank in the town center. I'd planned every step with Dimi and only withdrew enough cash to fly to the States and get settled."

"I often wondered about those secret meetings you had when Bianca and I weren't included."

"Now you know why. After showing the banker

my passport and the letter from my grandfather verifying the origin of the funds in my account, I took a taxi to the airport."

Her eyes lit up. "You really were free at last."

"Except that you weren't with me."

"Let's not talk about that. Tell me what happened next."

"I bought a one-way ticket to New York. As it took off, I saw the jet-d'eau at the end of Lake Geneva and the Alps in the distance. You know I'd traveled through Europe before and had been to Switzerland on several vacations. But this time everything was different."

Shadows marred her classic features. "I can't imagine it."

His body tautened. "That's when I realized I had left you behind for good. You wouldn't be able to come to me, nor I to go to you. My ache for you turned into excruciating pain." Hot tears stung his eyes. "Gemma—I swear I didn't know how I was going to be able to handle the separation."

Hers filled with tears, too, revealing the degree of her pain.

"You and I had grown up together and lived through everything. I was tortured by the knowledge that until the situation within my own family changed, our separation would have to be permanent."

"When I first heard you'd gone, I thought I was going to die."

He reached for her hand, enclosing it in his. "I would have given anything to spare you that pain. There was no way to know how soon we'd ever be able to see each other again."

She gave his hand a little squeeze before removing hers.

"You can't imagine my panic. I feared you would hate me forever for my inexplicable cruelty in telling you nothing. There'd be no way you could forgive me. But I didn't know how else to keep you safe from my father's wrath. To my sorrow, you didn't escape it entirely."

"You know what hurts the most, Vincenzo? To realize our teenage love wasn't strong enough in your mind to handle telling me the truth before you ever left Italy."

"I thought I was protecting you."

"I realize that now, but why did you lie to me again the other day about your reasons for leaving?"

"Again, I wanted to shield you from so much ugliness."

"Did you think I'm not strong enough to handle it?"

"I know you are, Gemma. Forgive me."

"Of course I do," she cried. "Finish telling me about New York."

"It was a different world. I checked into a hotel and called my grandfather Emanuele to let him know where I was, knowing he wouldn't tell my father. After talking with him, I phoned my grandfather in Padua to thank him for all he'd done for me...all he'd tried to do for my mother."

"He must have been so thrilled to hear from you."

"When he knew I had escaped, you should have heard him weep."

"Oh, Vincenzo. To think he'd lost his daughter at your father's hands. It's so terrible."

He could feel her grief. "It was over a long time ago, Gemma. Later I placed an ad in *Il Giorno*, needing to talk to Dimi. Four days later the call came. The first thing I demanded was to hear news of you!"

She'd buried her face in her hands. "What did he tell you?"

"Dimi couldn't give me any information. He said that while an intensive search of the countryside had been going on for me, he'd arranged to leave the *castello* that morning with Zia Consolata. He realized that if he didn't get them out of there, he would be my father's next victim."

"I can't bear it, Vincenzo."

"The news was devastating to me. He'd promised to watch out for you. Instead you were gone, and he had to leave, too."

"I'm so sad that you and your cousin will always carry those scars."

He took a deep breath. "I cringed to realize the suffering my disappearance had brought on everyone. And worse, knowing I couldn't comfort you. Neither could Dimi. He tried looking for you."

She dashed the tears from her eyes. "I can hardly stand to think about that time, but I have to know more. How *did* you survive when you got to New York? You'd never been there before."

Her interest thrilled him, because until he'd told her the truth, she'd refused to listen to anything.

"Don't forget I'd been making plans for a whole year. As soon as I arrived, I checked into a hotel Dimi and I had picked out, then had my funds electronically transferred from Switzerland to a bank in New

York. Two days later I applied to take the SAT college entrance test."

"You're kidding—"

His brows lifted. "You can't go to college without sending in the results."

He felt her eyes play over his features. "With your education, you must have been a top candidate."

"Let's just say I did well enough to get into NYU, but I didn't receive the results for eight weeks. During that waiting period, I purchased a town house in Greenwich Village."

"What was it like?"

"The architecture is nineteenth-century Greek Revival, with three bedrooms. I wanted to have enough room for Dimi when he was able to join me. But of course that never happened because he didn't want to move my aunt, who preferred being in her own palazzo."

"Of course. I'm so sorry. Tell me about the university. What courses did you take?"

"Business and finance classes. Thanks to my grandfather Nistri, who was my business model growing up, I started buying failing companies with his money and turning them around to sell for profit."

She let out a cry. "Nistri Technologies is your corporation!"

"One of them. My *nonno* was brilliant and taught me everything he knew. Little by little I started to build my own fortune and planned to pay him back every penny once I'd made the necessary money. But he died too soon for that to happen."

"You're a remarkable man." Her voice shook.

"No, Gemma. Just a lucky one to have had a

mother and grandfather like mine. He had a contact at NYU who taught an elite seminar for serious business students. This revered economics professor formed a think tank for his most ambitious followers and told us to visualize our greatest dreams."

"Is that where you met your friends?"

"*Si*. For different reasons, Takis and Cesare came to the States from Greece and Sicily to study and work. Like me, they wanted to make a lot of money. This seminar that brought us together was a complete revelation to the three of us. We grew close, and they went on to become wealthy, highly successful hotel and restaurant entrepreneurs."

"As did you. Why was this professor so effective?"

"No particular reason except he was brilliant. We learned it wasn't good enough to want to make money. You've got to know how to get it, how to deal with brokers, renovate, assess the value of property, how to buy, sell and secure a mortgage. He sounded just like my grandfather."

"Was that period of your life good for you?"

"Very good in some ways. Our mentor drummed into our heads how to cut costs, decide how much risk to assume in investments and balance our portfolios in order to impress anyone. His final rule was ingrained on my psyche. 'You must find out if your friends can be loyal.'"

"You and your partners must be very close."

"I trust them implicitly. That means everything. When I brought them together with my idea to buy the *castello*, I hadn't seen either of them in at least two months and had missed them. They got excited when I showed them pictures."

"There's no place like it." Her eyes glistened with unshed tears. "After the pain you and Dimi endured at the hands of your fathers, I'm glad you've found friends like that."

"So am I."

"When I met them, I didn't know they were owners and your partners. Both of them have made me feel comfortable. Some of the people in the culinary world are hard to deal with, but your friends aren't stuffy or full of themselves."

"So you like them?"

"I do. They have a lot of charm and sophistication. Before I knew what was going on, I thought that whoever owned this hotel knew what they were doing to employ them."

"They're the best, and they'll be pleased when I pass on what you said."

She cocked her head. "Do you mind answering another question for me?"

"Ask away."

"You may not be married yet, but is there someone waiting for you to return to New York?"

Vincenzo was in a mood to tell her the whole truth. "Yes and no."

He saw her swallow. "What do you mean?"

"I've been away from Annette five weeks this time. Yesterday on the phone she told me I sounded different. She wanted to know why. I told her about the Italian girl I fell in love with in my youth, the girl I hadn't seen or heard from in ten years until two days ago."

If he wasn't mistaken, he heard a moan pass her lips.

"I explained that meeting you was a complete ac-

cident. Annette wanted to know more. All I could tell
her was that a big portion of my past had just caught
up with me and I was still reeling. I know she wanted
more reassurance, but I couldn't give it to her."

She averted her eyes.

"What about you, Gemma? There has to be someone in your life." He braced himself for what might
be coming.

"I dated a little after moving to Florence. But the
only important relationship I had with a man was a
year ago."

The blood pounded in his ears. "Did you love
him?"

"I tried. My feelings for Paolo were different than
those for you, but I felt an attraction. He was a writer
for *Buon Appetito*, a nationwide food magazine, and
had covered the school for an article. His interview
with me turned into a date, and we started seeing
each other.

"After a month he wanted me to sleep with him. I
thought about it, hoping it would help me forget you,
but in the end I couldn't do it. He was very upset, so I
told him I couldn't go out with him anymore because
it wouldn't be fair to him. He accused me of loving
someone else even though I'd told him there'd been
no important man in my life for years."

Vincenzo's breath caught. He'd hoped for honesty
from her and her confession brought out his most
tender feelings. He now had his answer to why she'd
come to this particular restaurant tonight. Her ache
for him had grown worse, too. They suffered from
the same pain.

"Paolo said he wanted to marry me, but I told him

no because I didn't love him the way he needed to be loved. I couldn't even sleep with him. For both our sakes, I knew we had to stop seeing each other and get on with our separate lives. I'd lost my heart to the man I'd grown up with."

"Gemma…"

"After this long, it had to be unbearable to relive the ugly truth of your family's tragedy to me tonight, Vincenzo. Thank you for your courage, for forcing me to listen to the last page in the book. You were right. I needed to hear the ending so I can let go of my anger. Now I can close it."

This intimacy with Gemma, the knowledge that all the secrets were out, had changed his world forever. They'd been brought together again, and he loved her with every fiber of his being. The rush of knowing she'd been the constant heart in their relationship filled every empty space in his soul.

He grasped both her hands, ignited by the desire to be her everything. "Since we're past the age of eighteen, I have a simple solution to our problem that has been out there for the last ten years."

"What are you saying?"

"Marry me, Gemma."

With those words, everything changed in an instant.

A stillness seemed to envelope the room. Her complexion took on a distinct pallor that revealed more than she would ever know.

"A *duca* doesn't wed the cook."

Somehow he hadn't expected that response. He'd thought that because a miracle had brought them together at last, they'd gotten past every obstacle. After baring his soul to her, Vincenzo couldn't sit there any longer knowing she was more entrenched in that old world than he would have believed. She still saw him as the son of the evil *duca*. Like father, like son?

Cut to the quick, he let go of her hands and got to his feet. "This *duca* won't be a *duca* much longer. Enjoy the rest of your evening, *bellissima*."

He flew out of her flat to his car. As he accelerated down the road, he could hear her calling to him in the distance, but he didn't stop. After believing that telling her the truth would make them free to love each other as man and wife, the opposite had happened.

A duca *doesn't wed the cook.* The words that came out of her had been so cold, it frightened him. He felt as if the bottom had dropped out of his world once more. But by the time he'd pulled up to the front of the *castello*, his sanity had returned.

Vincenzo should have been ready for that automatic response—after all, Gemma had learned it from her mother at a very early age. He'd known how Mirella had always tried to guide Gemma and put distance between them because they were from different classes. But tonight his heart had been so full, he couldn't take the answer she'd thrown back at him.

The class divide was a more serious obstacle to a future with her than anything else. He planned to deal with that issue soon, but first he needed to leave for New York and take care of vital business. When he returned, he'd be able to concentrate on Gemma and their future. Because they *were* going to have one!

No sooner had Vincenzo gone than Gemma's phone rang. But she was so fragmented after her conversation with him, she ran into the other room and flung herself across the bed. Great heaving sobs poured out of her.

Something was wrong with her. Since the moment he'd entered Takis's office, appearing like a revenant, she seemed to have turned into a different person, one she didn't know. Nothing she'd said had come out right. Every conversation after that had ended in disaster. Either she ran out on him or he walked out on her.

Marry me, Gemma.

That's what he'd asked her moments ago. And what did she do? Throw his proposal back in his incredibly handsome face! *That's because you've been on the defensive from the moment he came back into your life, Gemma Rizzo!*

No wonder he'd walked out on her. Why wouldn't he? Didn't he know she loved him with all her heart and soul? But he was a *duca*. And that made a marriage between them out of the question, even though it was what she wanted more than anything in the world. While he'd been holding her hands, her body had throbbed with desire for him.

Gemma lay there out of her mind with a new kind of grief. All these years she'd misjudged him so terribly. Now the truth of his revelations burned hot inside her. At this point she knew she was more in love with him than ever.

But the woman who owned the *pensione* had recognized Vincenzo as the new Duca di Lombardi. That revelation was the coup de grâce for Gemma. His title created a chasm between them that could never be bridged. His marriage proposal thrilled her heart, but she couldn't marry him. In fact, everything was much worse.

While she worked at the *castello*, she would have to keep her distance from him. That she'd been crazy in love with him and they'd grown up spending as much time together as possible made it all the more difficult.

He had a potent charisma she found irresistible. Gemma didn't trust herself around him. Vincenzo had a way of crooking his finger and she'd come running no matter how hard she fought against it.

But she couldn't allow things to end this way. It was up to her to repair the damage and reason with him so he would understand. She hadn't told him that her mother didn't know about her new job yet. If Mirella had any idea he'd asked Gemma to marry him, there'd be even more grief, and Gemma didn't want to think about that.

Unfortunately it was too late to see him tonight. Tomorrow after work she'd find him and ask him if they could go somewhere private and talk this situation out.

After she'd cried until there were no tears left, she went to the bathroom to get ready for bed, then she returned Filippa's phone call. Her friend was excited because she'd received an affirmative response from one of the restaurants in Ottawa. "I'm flying to Canada tomorrow for the interview."

"That's wonderful." Gemma was thrilled for her. "Call me when you get there and tell me everything. Just think. You'll be closer to New York."

"It's very exciting. Now tell me, what's the situation on your end?"

"You don't want to know and I don't want to bur-den you when you're so happy."

"Let me be the judge of that."

Gemma spent the next while telling her all the shocking truths Vincenzo had revealed. "Although I've forgiven him, and I do understand, I'm still hurt he couldn't tell me the truth before."

"He was only eighteen, remember? And tonight he finally told you the whole truth."

"But you haven't heard it all yet. He's asked me to marry him."

"What?"

"Yes, and because I know a marriage to him is so impossible, I told him a *duca* doesn't marry the cook!"

"Oh, Gemma…you didn't! No wonder you're a mess."

"I am. During those early years we never had trou-ble communicating. Not ever."

"But you want something that isn't possible, be-cause you're not teenagers anymore."

"I was more sane as a teenager than I am now. For-give me for not making any sense tonight."

"You've been in shock since his return. I'm pretty sure he's in the same condition. Give it all time to sink in."

"I don't have another choice. Promise to call me from Canada and tell me everything."

"Don't worry. Now try to get a good sleep."

"I don't know if I can. Be safe, Filippa, and good luck!"

"Thanks. Be nice to Vincenzo. He could use it. Ciao."

Those words couldn't have made Gemma feel

guiltier, but she knew her friend hadn't intended any-thing hurtful. Quite the opposite, in fact. Filippa al-ways made good sense. With a plan in mind to talk to Vincenzo tomorrow, Gemma got ready for bed and was surprised she didn't have trouble falling asleep.

The next morning, she got up and ready for the day. With the formal meetings with the owners and staff out of the way, she dressed for regular work in a short-sleeved top and pleated pants rather than a skirt. Be-fore she left Sopri, she would buy a few groceries to put in the mini fridge for future meals. In fact, while she was shopping, she'd buy a pool lounger to take out to the lake behind the *castello*.

Until the opening of the hotel, she and Maurice would be working midmorning hours on menus and ordering the staples. But for a few more weeks there'd be free time in the afternoons before the intense work began and she earned her keep.

In the past there was nothing she'd enjoyed more than watching the swans, especially when Vincenzo had joined her. She assumed the water fowl were still there and would be an attraction for hotel guests. For now, she could lie in the sun and read a good thriller before leaving to drive back to the *pensione*. Maybe she could ask Vincenzo to meet her out there later in the day so they could really talk.

Though she followed through with her plans, she discovered that Vincenzo had flown to New York and wouldn't be back for a while. The news made her ill. She kept busy, but inside she was dying. He could have left Italy for personal as well as legitimate business reasons. She'd never know and speculation didn't get her anywhere.

Four days later she was in the depths of despair when she overheard Cesare and Takis talking in the kitchen. Vincenzo would be arriving at the airport at eight thirty that evening. She hugged the information to herself, trying not to react to her joy so anyone would notice.

After she finished the day's work with Maurice, she drove back to the *pensione* and kept busy until evening. Once she'd showered and changed into a sundress, she drove back to the *castello*. To her relief she saw the Maserati parked in front. Thankful Vincenzo was back safely, she hurried up the steps to find him.

One of the security men, Fortino, let her in the front entrance. This was the first time in ten years that she'd been here at night. The place was quiet as a tomb. Maybe because it was a Friday night and Vincenzo's partners had gone out. It was too early for anyone to be in bed. Gemma had no idea about their personal lives, though she remembered Vincenzo telling her that they were both single.

She wished she had his cell phone number, but he hadn't given it to her. If he wasn't in the kitchen, he might be out with Takis and Cesare. Then again, he was probably exhausted after his long flight and could be up in his tower room.

A long, long time ago, she'd gone looking for him there after hearing he'd suffered a terrible fall from his horse, or so she'd been told at the time. Desperate to make certain he was all right, she'd made her way to his aerie at the top of the *castello*, afraid one of his father's guards would see her. His door had been ajar and she'd heard him moan.

Summoning her courage tonight, she stole through the massive structure and made the same trek as before up the stone staircase at the rear. It wound round and round until she arrived at the forbidding-looking medieval iron door. This time it was closed. She held her breath while she listened for any sound.

Nothing came through except the pounding of her own heart.

Gemma knocked. "Vincenzo? Are you in there?" She waited.

Still no response.

It was here—away from everyone, away from any help—that Vincenzo's father had attacked him. A little sob escaped her lips to think something so terrible had happened to him. Yet he'd survived. She loved him desperately.

Desolate because he wasn't there, she turned to go back down when she heard the heavy door open behind her and whirled around.

"Gemma—" His deep male voice infiltrated her body. "What are you doing up here?" He was half-hidden by the door.

"I heard you were back from New York and I've been waiting to talk to you in private. I know it's late, but I need to apologize for my cruelty to you the last time we were together."

"Growing up I memorized your mother's views on class distinctions like a catechism. Your answer to my marriage proposal shouldn't have come as a surprise, although I'd hoped for a different response."

She bit her lip. "That's why I came up here. To talk about this like an adult."

"My problem is, I'm in an adult mood. If you cross over my threshold, I won't be accountable for my behavior. Is that honest enough for you?"

Thump, thump went her heart. "Vincenzo—I'm so sorry—"

"For what?"

"For throwing your proposal back in your face like I did."

"Are you saying you didn't mean it?"

"Yes—no—I mean—"

"You can't have it both ways," he broke in on her. "This isn't a black-and-white situation."

"So you admit there's some gray area where we can negotiate?"

She let out a troubled sigh. "I shouldn't have come up here."

"Are you saying good-night, then? I can assure you I'd much rather you came in my room the way you did a long time ago, but the decision is up to you."

Close to a faint from wanting to be with him, she turned to go back down the stairs. The next thing she knew, Vincenzo had caught her around the waist with his strong arms. *"Oh—"*

"Is this what you want, Gemma? Yes or no?"

Heaven help her. "Yes—"

CHAPTER SEVEN

VINCENZO PULLED HER into his room so her back was crushed against his chest.

"After our troubled reunion days ago, I didn't expect a welcome home like this. I love this dress, by the way. You're not so covered up." He kissed her neck, sending curls of delight through her body.

There was a playful side to him that seduced her. Though he was still dressed in trousers, Gemma could tell he was shirtless. His male scent and the faint aroma of the soap he used were intoxicating. She struggled for breath. "I didn't know if you were up here or not."

"I'd barely arrived and was getting ready to drive to the *pensione* to find you." He buried his face in her hair like he'd done so many times in the past. "You have no idea how beautiful you are. I couldn't get back fast enough. When did you let this profusion of silk grow out?"

"Mamma liked it short, but I got tired of the style."

"It's breathtaking and smells divine."

He'd always said wonderful things to her. "I don't remember your voice being this deep."

His low chuckle excited her. "Yours is the same."

"I think you're taller than you once were."

"So are you, in high heels. I don't think I ever told you how much I love your long legs." He turned her around so he could look into her eyes. "Do you think we're through growing up?"

In the dim glow of a lamp she saw a glimmer of a smile hover at the corners of his compelling mouth.

"I don't know. You're still the tease I remember."

"And you still blush. Give me your mouth, Gemma, so I'll know not everything has changed."

She put her hands against his chest with its dusting of black hair. "Please don't kiss me again, Vincenzo. I was simply trying to find you so I could explain what I meant the other night after you followed me to the *pensione* to talk. Everything came out wrong. I'll go downstairs while you finish getting dressed and meet you in the lobby, where we can have the conversation we should have had."

Gemma tried to pull away from him, but he held her firmly in his grasp. "The last time you came to this room, I had to let you go too soon because I was afraid you could be in danger. That's not the case anymore, and I've waited too long for this moment."

He lowered his mouth to hers and began kissing her. A kiss here, a kiss there, then one so long and deep her legs started to give way. Vincenzo picked her up in his arms and carried her past the square hunting table in front of the fireplace to the hand-carved bed.

The suite had been redecorated in nineteenth-century decor with every accoutrement befitting his title. But Gemma wasn't aware of anything except this man who was kissing her senseless. No longer the eighteen-year-old she'd adored, he was a man already making her feel immortal.

When she'd come to his bed ten years ago, he'd been suffering, in pain, and they'd had to be so careful how they kissed and held each other. Not wanting to make it worse, Gemma had had to be the one to make it easier for him to get close to her and caress her.

Tonight that wasn't their problem. With one kiss Vincenzo had swept her away to a different place, exciting her in ways she hadn't thought possible. He rolled her over so he could look down at her. His hands roamed her hips and arms as if memorizing her.

"I could eat you alive, *bellissima*." He kissed every feature of her face before capturing her mouth again and again. One kiss turned into another, drowning her in desire. Vincenzo was such a gorgeous man, she couldn't believe he was loving her like this. "I know this is what you want, too. You can't deny it. You're in my blood and my heart, Gemma."

"You're in mine," she cried softly. "I can't remember a moment when you weren't a part of me."

"I want you with me. It's past time we were together."

She cupped his striking face in her hands. "That's what you say now."

He kissed the tips of her fingers. "What kind of a comment is that? You think I'm going to change? Wouldn't I have already done that over the years we've been apart? I've already asked you to marry me. What more proof do you need? That's a commitment to last forever." He plundered her mouth with another heart-stopping kiss.

Gemma moaned. "All lovers say that. If you were a normal man, I could believe it."

He raised up on one elbow, tracing the outline of her lips. "You don't think I'm normal? We've been apart too long. Spend the night with me and you'll find out the truth."

"I don't mean that kind of normal, and you know it."

"With you lying here in my arms, your lambent green eyes as alive with desire as your body, I'm in the mood to humor you. I hunger for you, Gemma."

"You're not thinking clearly, Vincenzo." She fought tears. "I can't marry you."

Lines marred his arresting features. "Of course you can. A *duca* can do whatever he likes, choose whatever woman he wants, just like any other man."

"I know," she whispered, turning her head away. Oh, how well she knew after learning the dark secrets inside the walls of the *castello*. His father's and uncle's proclivities for other women had been one of the great scandals in all Lombardi.

He caught her chin so she had to look at him. "Let's get something straight once and for all. I have despised the class system all my life and fought against it growing up. The idea of finding the right princess to marry in order to gain more power and money is revolting to me. Your love sustained me growing up. It means more to me than any riches or possessions."

She eased away from him and sat up, smoothing the hair off her forehead. "You say that now."

"I'll say it now and until the end of our days together."

"Vincenzo—" A sob escaped. "You just don't understand."

"Then help me." He tugged on her hand so she couldn't get off the bed. She'd never heard him sound so dark.

"You're the most wonderful, remarkable man I've ever known. But you were born with a special destiny."

"No. I happened to be born the son of a *duca*. That's not destiny. It's an accident of birth."

"Please listen. I'm going to tell you something you never knew. One time when your grandfather was out in the back courtyard in his wheelchair, I was sent out to take him a sweet. He loved Mamma's zeppole. I gave them to him.

"After he thanked me, I started to hurry away, but he called to me. 'Come back here, *piccola*,' he said and reached for my hand. 'I've seen you with my grandson. You've been a good friend to him and I can tell you like him. And I know why. Can you keep a secret?' I nodded.

"'There's a reason everyone likes him. One day he'll grow up to be the finest *duca* of us all. With his princess he'll raise future *duchi*, who will have a wonderful father to look up to. But I'm afraid I won't live to see it.' He kept hold of my hand and wept.

"Even though I was young, I realized that he was letting me know how lucky I was to be in your company. When I ran back to Mamma and told her, she said it was a sign from heaven that I should always respect my friendship with you. To think of wanting anything more would be sacrilege."

* * *

"*Santa Madre di Dio!*" Vincenzo got off the bed, putting his hands on his hips in a totally male stance. "So
that's the reason for all this talk! Gemma—if it will
ease your mind, I've heard your opinion on the subject before. Your mother shared her beliefs because
she loves you and wants to protect you."

"Still, my temper sometimes gets the best of me."

"I remember," he murmured. "That time you and
Bianca went swimming in the lake without your
clothes. You thought Dimi and I had been spying on
you and had taken them. I confess we did spy with
my binoculars from a tree at the edge of the forest."

"Vincenzo—"

"But it turned out we weren't the culprits. The dog
of one of the guards ran off with your clothes. We
chased it down and brought your things back to you,
but I don't recall you thanking us."

She shook her head. "We were too embarrassed
to talk. That was so humiliating, you can't imagine."

"You were our wood nymphs come to life. Dimi
and I thought it was the most wonderful day we'd
ever spent."

"You would!" But even across the expanse sepa-
rating them he detected a half smile.

"I'll tell you another secret. My mother was very
fond of you. But because she was a princess, she believed any feelings I had for you would come to grief.
Like your mother, Mamma had also been raised in
a different world of rigidity within the titled class."

Gemma sat on the edge of the bed. "Her words
were prophetic."

"Not completely. Dimi and I broke rules all over

the place. It's a new world now. Because of a reaction to the misuse of noble titles in our country, you'll notice a trend among legitimate aristocracy in this last decade to refrain from making use of their titles."

"I didn't realize."

"What's important is that you and I have found each other again and I'm no longer in danger from my father or uncle. The powers that be are gone."

"Thank heaven for that, Vincenzo. But what did you mean when you said you wouldn't be a *duca* much longer?"

He hadn't meant to tell her this soon, but right now he was desperate to get closer to her. "Since my return to Italy, there are men in the government who know of my business interests in the US and here. I'm not blind. Because of my title they want me to get on board with them to play an economic role in the region's future. It's all political, Gemma. The title corrupted my father and uncle. It turned their souls dark. I refuse to let that happen to me."

"You don't know if the title did that to them, Vincenzo. I watched you grow up titled, remember? I never once saw you do an unkind thing in your whole life." She stared hard at him. "You can't change who you are."

"Oh, but I can."

"How?"

"By renouncing my title. Once that's done, it's permanent. If I have a son or sons, they won't inherit it, and any daughters I might have can't inherit it anyway. The beauty of it is that an Italian title of nobility cannot be sold or transferred. In other words, the abuse stops with me. My male children and their children and the children after them won't be burdened."

Her eyes widened. "If you do that, won't the title fall on Dimi through his father?"

"Yes, but he's taking the same steps."

"You'd both stop the title from progressing after centuries of succession?"

Vincenzo nodded. "There are so many dreadful things my father and uncle did in the name of that title, seen not only in the scars that Dimi and I carry. You know the head gardener who was introduced at the orientation meeting?"

"Yes. I met him out in back the first day."

"Years ago, my father got angry at him for planting some flowers Mamma wanted. He told him to get out and never come back. He didn't give him a reference or any severance pay. While Dimi and I were looking up old employees, we found him.

"That's just one of a hundred stories I could tell you of my father's cruelty. If he and my uncle hadn't been born to a *duca*, they wouldn't have felt they had the right to treat people like animals. The only way to end the corruption is to rid ourselves of the title and restore the honor of those noble Gagliardis from the past by preserving the *castello*."

"*That's* why you turned it into a resort," she whispered.

"What better way to make restitution than by allowing the public to enjoy its heritage, thereby giving back something good and decent to the region."

Her features sobered. "You loved your grandfather Emanuele. He was a great *duca*. How would he feel about this?"

"I can't speak for him, but if he's looking down on us now, he couldn't be pleased with what his sons did while he was dying. Being born with a title gives some men dangerous ideas."

"But not you, Vincenzo. Emanuele adored you. I don't think he'd want you to do this."

He frowned and got to his feet. "For someone who came close to bearing the brunt of my father's dark side, I'm surprised to hear this coming from you. I thought you of all people would be happy to see this kind of inequality come to an end."

"But you're a different breed of man and shouldn't have to give up what is part of you."

"I'm a man, pure and simple. Don't endow me with anything else. This isn't an idea I just came up with on a whim. When I was five, maybe six, I saw my father kick one of the young stable hands to the ground because he didn't call him Your Highness. It sickened me. That was the day my plan was born. Now I can see it through to fruition."

The way she shook her head filled him with consternation. What could he say to get through to her?

"Years ago I told you I'd find a way for us to be married. A few days ago I asked you to be my wife because there'd be no barrier between us. But there *is* one. It goes so much deeper than I realized."

His words caused her to flinch, alarming him.

"When you said you and I weren't the same people growing up, I didn't understand how fully you meant it." His chest felt tight. "It's clear you don't love me the same way I love you, no matter what I do. I can tell you would rather I keep the title, the very thing you think prevents us from ever getting married."

He started pacing in frustration, then stopped. "Is this because of what my *nonno* said? It's no wonder you don't think you can marry me."

"I didn't mean to upset you. I thought if I told you about that experience, you would begin to see."

"I see, all right," he muttered. "Mirella deliberately interpreted it so you would only worship me from afar. She didn't want you getting any ideas about a real relationship with the future *duca*. After all this time, it's still working."

"You can scoff about this all you want, Vincenzo, but it was very serious to me. He was a prayerful man. I saw him go to Mass in the private *castello* chapel every day before I left for school."

"He wasn't a priest destined to be cardinal one day, Gemma. Who do you think administered the Mass to him every morning?"

"You don't have to be a priest to be a godly person. Everyone felt that way about the old *duca*. I know you loved him."

"That's beside the point. He knew he was dying. All he was doing that day was expressing his sentiment about me to a sweet girl who'd brought him his favorite dessert baked by the best cook around. But to see that as a sign from above…" He shook his head.

Gemma slid off the bed. "My mother was raised in a good Catholic family."

He raked a hand through his midnight-black hair. "Heaven help me, so were you."

"That's why she honored the traditions here."

"You're right, but she went too far. Without giving me any voice at all, she made me out as the un-touchable one, the future *duca* whose word was law.

It's that old divine right of kings business and it disgusts me."

No one could confuse her like he could with his logic.

"It's time to put the past *in* the past, where it belongs. There's no room in the modern world for it. I'm a normal guy, Gemma. Warts and all."

"You don't have any."

Vincenzo leaned against the door with his strong arms folded. "Of course I have flaws and imperfections, like every other man. Think about it—until I called my friends together about buying the *castello*, they didn't know my last name or the fact that I inherited a title. Do you see them treating me any differently? Have they once shown me a special kind of deference?"

"Actually, no," she said with her innate honesty.

"Good. Maybe that will convince you. Please hear me out. We need to be spending time together as adults, not as those teenagers from the past having to live by ridiculous rules that constantly divided us in your mind. It's important—in fact, it's *vital*—that you throw away the blinders while we explore the world we're living in now as equals in all things and ways."

Gemma could hear what he was saying, but it was so hard to silence her mother's warnings after all these years. It meant throwing off old fears and conceptions that had dominated her thoughts forever.

"I'm in love with you. Isn't it worth it to you to find out if you can see me as a typical man you've met and want to get to know better?"

Vincenzo was the most atypical man she'd ever

known, but he couldn't see it. He wasn't a woman. She hugged her arms to her waist. "You already know what's in my heart."

"I do?" he quipped, making her smile. "Then prove it. Here's what we're going to do."

She recognized that no-nonsense tone in his voice. When he went after something, he was impossible to stop. Gemma knew she had to get away from him. "There's nothing to do, Vincenzo. I have to leave."

With a few long strides, he stood in the front of the doorway so she couldn't walk out. He was such a breathtaking male, her legs turned to mush.

"The second I learned you didn't have a husband, I planned for us to take a vacation together. That's why I left that night for New York. There were loose ends I needed to tie up first so we wouldn't have anything standing in our way."

"That's a fantasy you need to let go of. For one thing, you just employed me. I can't take a vacation."

"There's still enough time before the grand opening for us to be gone a couple of weeks. My partners will handle everything, and you've already done the most important work with Maurice. When was the last time you went off on a real trip anywhere? Be honest."

Her eyes closed tightly. "I don't remember."

"That's what I thought. I need a holiday badly, too, but I never felt like taking one because the woman I wanted with me wasn't available. My fear that you were happily married and living somewhere in Italy with your husband and children tortured me more nights than you'll ever know."

Gemma had battled the same fears about him and had suffered endlessly for years.

"We'll leave in the morning. Go home and get packed. I'll come by the *pensione* at eight. We'll drive to the airport and have breakfast on the plane."

He was serious. It frightened and thrilled her at the same time. She moistened her lips. "Aren't you too tired to go anywhere after coming back from New York?"

"When we get to the beach, we'll sleep, relax and play in the water to our hearts' content."

It did sound out of this world.

"If—if we go," she stammered, "I don't want us to sleep together. When we're in each other's arms we communicate as a man and woman, but—"

"We certainly do."

Heat filled her cheeks. "You know what I mean. I didn't think of you as the *duca* while we were on the bed, but at other times—"

"I get where you're going with this," he broke in. "You want to see us as that man and woman no matter what else we're doing."

She nodded.

"So do I, so I'll try to keep my hands off you. But I'll warn you now, it's not going to be easy." He walked over to the massive dresser and pulled out a knit shirt he put on. "I thought I'd better cover up before I walk you out to your car. Fortino's a man and would understand, but I don't want him to get the wrong idea about you."

"Thank you."

His deep chuckle reverberated through her body as he caught her face between his hands, kissing her long and hard. Like old times, they wrapped their arms around each other and started down the winding staircase. Vincenzo stopped every so often to give her another kiss. She didn't think they'd ever reach the bottom and didn't care.

They crossed through the *castello* to the front entrance. "It feels like we're the only two people on earth."

"Don't I wish," he whispered against her throat. They nodded to Fortino and went down to her car. "Let's exchange phones so we can put in our numbers. I want you to call me the second you reach the *pensione*."

She nodded. When that was done, he crushed her against him. "*Ci vediamo domattina.*"

If she wasn't dreaming, then she would be seeing him in the morning. Taking the initiative, she pressed a kiss to his lips and climbed in the car. "Tomorrow."

Vincenzo packed a bag, then phoned his cousin before getting in bed. "Dimi?"

"Are you back from New York?"

"Yes, and I'm going away again, but I wanted to call you first. How's Zia Consolata?"

"Failing a little more each day."

"I'm so sorry. When I get back from this trip, I'll come and spend a few days with her to give you some relief."

"Where are you going?"

"I've had a breakthrough with Gemma." He'd always told his cousin everything. For the next little while he explained what had gone on this evening.

The part about her conversation with their grandfather Emanuele came as a shock to him.

"You're right. That gave Mirella more ammunition. But I'm worried. You sound too excited, Vincenzo. The zebra doesn't lose its stripes."

Vincenzo didn't want to hear that. "But she has agreed to go on vacation with me."

"Just be warned. You've been in hell for years. Two weeks with her might still not be enough to make her see the light."

His breath caught. "Thanks for your optimism."

"I just don't want you to end up in more pain that could last for the rest of your life."

He didn't want that, either, and worried about his cousin. Vincenzo wished there was more he could do for him. Dimi had relationships with various women, but his prime concern was to take care of his mother.

"I love you for caring, Dimi. Talk to you soon. Ciao."

CHAPTER EIGHT

WHEN MORNING CAME Vincenzo dressed in chinos and a sport shirt, then met early with Cesare and Takis to tell them his plans. With everything settled, he phoned Gemma to say that he was on his way to Sopri in one of the hotel service vehicles. He'd parked his Maserati around the back of the *castello*.

When he pulled up in front, she came out with her suitcase. His heart rate picked up speed. She looked fabulous in white sailor pants and a sleeveless white top. He wondered how long it would be before the sight of her didn't send adrenaline pounding through his blood.

He jumped out of the car to help her in and put her case in the back. Those luscious lips of coral were too much of an enticement. By the time he'd finished kissing her, there was no more lipstick left.

"The *padrona* was watching out her window."

"Are you ever going to stop worrying about being with me?"

Her chest heaved. "I promise to try not to let my fears get the best of me."

"That's all I can ask." He tucked some strands of honey-blond hair behind her ear.

"Where are we going?"

"First we'll fly to someplace I haven't been before. Have you ever traveled to Bari along the Adriatic?"

"No."

"Good. I want to explore the coast."

"Ooh. That sounds exciting. Are we taking the ducal private jet?"

"No. We're flying commercial, like two ordinary people."

Her head turned toward him. "Are you teasing me?"

"Does that mean you're disappointed?"

She blushed. "Of course not."

"We're simply two people on holiday together, doing whatever we feel like."

By two in the afternoon, they'd arrived at Bari international airport and rented a car. Vincenzo was starting to feel in the holiday mood. They stopped at a deli to buy some wine and a bag of Italian sausage and egg pies.

He looked over at her. "Having a good time?"

"This is the best. Can you imagine how much fun we would have had if you'd been able to drive us around years ago?"

"I've tried hard not to imagine what joy that would have been. In truth, if I'd driven off in a car with you, no one would have seen us again. My father knew that if I got behind the wheel of any car, I'd disappear."

"No, you wouldn't have. Like you told me, you'd never leave your mother."

He squeezed her thigh. She remembered everything.

"When did you learn to drive?"

"After I got to New York and bought my first car."

"What kind?"

"A white Sentra, perfect for a college guy. I have pictures I'll show you."

"I want to see and know everything that happened to you."

"We've got the rest of our lives, Gemma."

She didn't respond, but he wasn't worried. She'd come with him and today was only the first day. They whizzed along, chatting and eating. They explored Puglia before coming to the medieval town of Polignano a Mare, scattered with white buildings.

"Oh, look, Vincenzo. This whole area is built on sheer cliffs."

"This is where we're staying tonight. Years ago the guys told me about this place. I've been anxious to see it ever since." He turned in to the Grotta Palazzese Hotel built from the local stone. "We can't see it from here, but there's a cave restaurant below where we're going to eat tonight."

"I've heard about it. I can't wait to see it! A real cave."

"Yes. Seventy or so feet above the water. Let's check in and get our room, then walk around some of those narrow streets until we get hungry."

Gemma's heart raced when Vincenzo asked the concierge for a key to their room. Except for the night she'd crept up to his room all those years ago, and last night, she'd never been in another man's bedroom.

There were several couples checking in. She wished she could be nonchalant about their situation. After they reached their room and closed the door, Vincenzo put their bags down and pulled her into his arms. They kissed hungrily.

"Relax. It'll get easier." He knew everything going on inside her. "Go ahead and freshen up." She passed the queen-size bed on the way to the bathroom. This was all so new to her, she had to pinch herself.

Before long he took her out to play tourist. She had the time of her life as they meandered through the ancient streets hand in hand. No woman they passed could take their eyes off Vincenzo. One of the clerks in a tourist shop fell all over herself to get his attention.

But he'd fastened his attention on Gemma. He constantly teased and kissed her all the way back to the hotel, where they dressed for dinner. In their youth they'd had to plan every move to be together so no one would find out. It had been as if they were caged. Little could she have imagined a night like this with him. To be free and open to show their love was intoxicating.

A cry escaped her lips when they went down the steps to the limestone cave restaurant below. In the twilight, the individual tables had been lit with candles. The whole ambience had a surreal feeling with the warm evening breeze coming off the Adriatic.

They were shown to a table for two and served an exquisite meal of prawns and swordfish. She looked into his silvery eyes. "You can hear the water lapping beneath us. This is an enchanting place."

"The guys were right. You can't find a more romantic spot anywhere in Italy."

"I agree. A restaurant without walls. It's incredible." Near the end of their meal, the waiter came over. "No more wine for me," she said. "One glass is all I can handle."

Vincenzo declined a second glass, too. "Shall we take a little walk before going to bed?"

The thought of being with him all night sent a wave of delight through her body. "I'd love it."

An hour later they returned to the hotel and headed for their room. Vincenzo waited for her to get ready for bed. While he was in the bathroom, she climbed under the covers, dressed in the only long nightgown she owned. She wasn't quite as full now, but the food had stimulated her. She doubted she'd be able to sleep at all lying next to him.

He entered the darkened room in his robe and opened the window to let in the sea air. When he got into bed, he turned on his side toward her and drew her around so she faced him.

"Do you know that since we've been together again, all we've done is concentrate on me? I want to talk about you. I want to hear everything that happened to you from the morning you had to leave the *castello*."

She tucked her hands beneath her pillow so she wouldn't be tempted to throw them around his neck. "That was the worst moment of our lives. Mamma was so quiet I was frightened. We left with Bianca and her mother in a taxi early in the morning. At the train station in Milan, we all said goodbye. They were going back to Bellinzona in Switzerland, where their family came from."

He let out a groan. "So that's why Dimi couldn't find her, either."

"I cried for days. Bianca and I promised to write,

but it didn't last very long, because they moved again and one of my letters came back saying *return to sender.*"

Vincenzo stroked her hair with his free hand.

"As for Mamma, she at least had her sister and niece in Florence. They offered us a home over the bakery. I loved them and we were very blessed, really. She was able to work in the bakery immediately to start earning money."

"Thank heaven your aunt was so good to you. I'd give anything to make it up to your mother for the pain. Not only couldn't I protect my own mother, I couldn't do a thing for yours."

Gemma heard the tears in his voice. "Please don't worry about it. My aunt knew Mamma had to use the Bonucci name so your father couldn't track her down. Everything worked out.

"On our first weekend there, Mamma took me to the cemetery to see my *papà*'s grave. I never knew him, so all I could feel was sadness for that. But for the first time in years, I watched her break down sobbing. I'd been so fixated on my own problems, I never realized how much she'd suffered after losing my father.

"Their married life had been cut short and she didn't have any more babies to love. My selfishness had caught up to me and I determined to be a better daughter to her from then on."

"You were the best, Gemma! I was always impressed by how close you were to her. How did you end up going to cooking school? You never talked about it to me. I didn't know that's what you wanted to do."

"I didn't, either. I assumed I'd to go college. One time when you and I were together, I told you as much in order to impress you."

"After I went to New York, I'd hoped that was what you would do."

"The trouble was, I didn't know what I wanted to study. Two weeks after we got to Florence, the family sat me down. I sensed they were worried about me, and they said they thought I might have been suffering from depression."

Vincenzo reached for one of her hands and kissed the palm.

"They told me I should attend cooking school. If I didn't like it, I didn't have to keep going. But since I'd already learned how to cook by watching Mamma, I'd be way ahead of the other students applying there.

"It sounded horrible to me, but everything sounded horrible back then." Her eyes stung with tears. "I'd lost all my friends."

"That's exactly how I felt when I arrived in New York," he whispered.

"Oh, Vincenzo—" She tried not to cry. "Over the years Mamma had saved a little money, but not enough to go toward my schooling. Yet I never felt deprived."

"You were loved, and that kind of wise frugality puts the sins my father and uncle committed to shame. Now keep telling me how you became a cook."

"So my aunt who runs the bakery knew someone in the administration at the Epicurean School, and I was given a scholarship. When she said that it was close enough for me to take the bus there, I realized they were all telling me I had to go and try it. I knew it was what my mother wanted. She'd sacrificed everything for me, so I did it."

"Did you hate it in the beginning?"

"No."

He smiled. "That's interesting."

"It was a surprise to my family, too. On the first day I met a girl named Filippa Gatti, who was from Florence. She reminded me of Bianca, and we became friends right away. She said she was tired of academic studies and wanted to do something different. After buying an expensive slice of ricotta cheese pie that tasted nasty, she thought, 'Why not be a pastry cook? Anyone could cook better than this!'"

"Why not?" Vincenzo laughed.

"With so many classes together, we hit it off, hating some of the teachers, loving others."

"You mean the same way Dimi and I felt about our tutors."

"Exactly."

"I'd like to meet her one day."

"She'd pass out if she ever met you."

"Ouch."

Gemma chuckled. "You know what I mean. There's no man like you around anywhere." He kissed her again. "She helped me deal with my pain over losing you, and our friendship got me through those nine years as an apprentice."

"I'm glad you have her in your life."

"So am I. You'd love her. She's darling, with black hair like yours and the most amazing sapphire-blue eyes. She's fun and *so* smart. After work we'd go to movies and eat dinner out and shop. Sometimes we took little trips along the Ligurian coastline. We'd visit lots of restaurants and check out the food."

He grinned. "Were there any good ones?"

"I found out you can't get a bad meal in Italy, but we determined to invent some fabulous dishes that would become famous someday. The truth is, Mamma was the creator in our family, better than my aunt or my grandmother and great-grandmother, who started the bakery. All I could do was try to match her expertise."

"You've succeeded, Gemma. Is Filippa as good a cook as you?"

"Much better, and that's the truth. She's innovative, you know?"

"I saw your résumé. You were named the top student in your class."

"That's because Signora Gallo, the woman on the board, loved my aunt and knew it would make her happy to give her niece the top ranking. It should have been Filippa."

"Where is she now?"

"In Canada, applying for a pastry chef position in Ottawa."

"Could you have applied there?"

"Yes, but I wanted a position in France. That is, until I saw the opening advertised at the *castello*."

"It was our luck we got you first. Finders, keepers. Cesare believes you applied for the position because it was meant to be. But I hope your friend gets what she wants."

"Me too. She always wanted to work at a restaurant in New York City and be written up in some glossy magazine as Italy's greatest cooking sensation. I'm kidding. She never said that, but I know she wanted to work in New York. In time I know she will, and I hope she becomes famous."

"I could put in a good word for her with Cesare. He owns an excellent restaurant chain."

She put her fingers to his lips. "No favors. We're going to be ordinary people right now, remember? But thank you for being so kind and generous."

"Gemma...an ordinary person can recommend someone for a job without being a *duca*."

"You don't know Filippa. She's intensely proud. The only way she would take a job would be for her to prove she's the very best at what she does. To be given a chance through a friend wouldn't go down with her at all."

"Sounds like your soul mate."

"Vincenzo—"

"Does she have a boyfriend who's going to miss her?"

"She *had* one. He let her down in a big way, but she's over the worst of it now."

"That's good. Now come here and let me kiss you the way I've been wanting to. We've talked long enough."

"I don't dare."

"Then will you do me a favor and turn on your other side? I can't promise not to reach out for you during the night. I have no idea what I do in my sleep."

"Then we're both in trouble. *Buonanotte*, Vincenzo. I've had the most wonderful day of my life."

"Guess what? We have two weeks of wonderful

days and nights ahead. Tomorrow I thought we'd fly to the island of Mykonos."

"You're joking. Aren't you?"

"Is that excitement I hear in your voice?"

"Yes! I've never been to Greece."

"Neither have I. Ironic, isn't it? I've traveled all over North and South America, parts of Asia. I've been to many of the states in the US—Hawaii, Alaska—and I know New York City like the back of my hand. But the rest of my education is still lacking."

"So is mine," Gemma murmured after she'd taken in what he'd just told her about his travels.

"Both Takis and Cesare say I have to see the Greek islands. Once you go there, you'll never want to travel anywhere else. I've arranged for us to stay at a small hotel with a restaurant, Gemma. It's on a white sandy beach where the waters are blue and crystal clear. You step right out of the room onto the beach. If you want, you can walk to town from there."

She let out a long sigh, picturing the white Greek architecture. "In my opinion, to live and be surrounded by water is true paradise. That's the one thing missing in Milan and Florence. They're both landlocked. Eating by the sea tonight inside that grotto was sheer enchantment. No other restaurant could compare."

"Being with you made it magical. Tomorrow morning we'll fly straight from Bari to Paxos. Sleep well, *il mio adorabile cuoca*." He leaned over to give her a tender kiss, then rolled on his other side.

Vincenzo had just called her his adorable cook.

"You're too good to me, you know. I haven't done anything for you but cause you trouble."

"If you want to make it up to me, all you have to say are four little words besides *I love you*."

I know.

"We're doing fine, aren't we? We're a man and a woman enjoying life together, right?"

"Yes." Her voice wobbled.

"You sound like you're going to cry."

"How do you know me so well?"

"Maybe because we met from the moment we were out of the cradle. You're as familiar to me as Dimi. No one else was in my world. I saw you in every mood and circumstance, just as you saw me."

"Our deep friendship is unique. On the strength of it, will you tell me the truth about something? When you went back to New York this time, did you see Annette?"

"Yes. We went to dinner and I told her she wouldn't be seeing me again because I was so madly in love with you, it was as if we'd never been apart."

"But—"

"No buts, Gemma. I can read your mind. If you can't commit to me by the end of our vacation, my feelings for Annette won't be resurrected. I can't imagine being a good husband to any woman when my heart has been yours from the age of five."

Now the tears started.

"Maybe that was the problem with my father and my uncle. Both of their marriages were arranged. They didn't have the luxury of already being in love with the women chosen for them. Our poor mothers had no choice, either."

"But they had you and Dimi to love."

"Still, what a shame they weren't lucky enough

to have grown up with the sweetest little girl on the planet. If I had to look for a reason for their notorious philandering, that might be one of them. I'd have fought dragons for you."

"I would have nursed your wounds." Her words came out ragged.

"That's what you did the night you came to my room. I ought to be thankful for what my father did to me. Though you didn't know he was the reason I was hurt, the news brought you to me."

"I still can't believe what he was capable of."

"It's over, and we were able to have that precious time together before I had to leave the country. The memory of that night was the only thing that has gotten me through the years—and Dimi, of course."

"Has he met a woman he loves?"

"He's had girlfriends, but no one special. My uncle is still alive and in prison. Work is Dimi's panacea to stave off the demons. With his contacts and resources, he's helped us put the details of the *castello* transaction together. He and the guys have developed a strong friendship already."

"You can't help but love Dimi. I've missed him terribly. Does he ever go to see his father?"

"Not yet. He's does a lot of his business at home to be with my aunt. She has several health care workers who provide relief for him. He says her doctor doesn't give her much longer to live."

"How hard for him. How hard for you. Forgive me for talking my head off."

"It's music I'll never grow tired of, Gemma. We were parted by too many years of silence. I'm greedy for all the time I can get with you."

She lay there bombarded by shock waves of feelings and emotions. Gemma didn't need any more time to know she wanted to be his wife. She'd always wanted to belong to him. What she had to do now was believe that even if he was the *duca*, he would stay this normal man who made her feel so complete she could die of happiness.

In that regard every woman wanted to believe that about the man she married. She wanted proof that he would always love her and never change. But no power on earth could give you proof like that. Her faith in him had to be enough. She *did* have faith in this man. Since she'd been with him again, it had been restored to new heights.

He's back now, Gemma.

He's back now, so what are you going to do about it?

Ten days playing on the beach beneath the Grecian sun had turned both of them into bronzed facsimiles of themselves. The shiny hair on Vincenzo's wood nymph reflected golden highlights that hadn't been visible before their trip. He never tired of watching Gemma or the voluptuous mold of her body.

She lay in the late-afternoon light on a lounger by the pool wearing a new turquoise-and-blue bikini.

"We've invented a new phrase, Gemma. Beach potatoes."

She lowered the thriller she was reading and broke into serious laughter, the kind he remembered from long ago. The nervous, worried woman he'd started out with on their flight to Bari was no longer visible. He loved this new Gemma, who seemed care-free and relaxed.

But she hadn't broken down, letting him know she wanted him to make love to her. The signs that she was ready to give him the answer he was waiting for hadn't come.

The zebra doesn't lose its stripes. Dimi's warning had haunted him throughout the night.

He'd decided to speak his mind now. There was no sense in putting it off, especially since the phone call he'd just received from Dimi.

Their loungers were placed side by side. She turned her head toward him. "I can see that look on your face."

"What look is that?"

"The one that says you've got something important to say."

"I can't hide much from you, can I?"

"Do you want to?" Her anxious question startled him. Well, well…beneath her calm facade she wasn't calm at all.

"No, Gemma. I was teasing. What I wanted to tell you was that while you were out in the sea a few minutes ago, Dimi phoned me."

"I didn't realize." She looked alarmed. "Is your aunt worse?"

"No. He called me because he just got word that my uncle died of liver failure in prison last night. They rushed him to the hospital, but it was too late."

Gemma sat up and slid her feet to the patio. "I hardly know what to say."

"That makes two of us."

"I'm sure he needs you right now."

Vincenzo nodded. "I've already made the flight arrangements for morning. When we reach Milan, we'll drive to his villa."

"In that case I'd better start getting packed."

"Wait—before you go in the room, there's something else I must tell you. I've been hoping you'd break down and talk to me about the thing I want most to hear. Since you haven't, I've decided you need another nudge."

"I don't understand," she cried softly.

"I'm renouncing the title right away. My uncle's death convinces me even more it's the right thing to do. Now Dimi and I can wipe the slate clean and be done with it. Even your mother would approve and give you her blessing. I'm looking forward to talking to her."

A gasp escaped her lips.

"Why the consternation? It's what you've always wanted so we could be together. Deep down it's what I've wanted, too. These days with you have been the happiest of my life. I'm not going to let anything change that now."

He got up from the lounger to pick up the towels and carry them into the room. She followed with the sunscreen and her book, but when he looked at her, she reminded him of a person suffering from shellshock. Good! The situation couldn't go on this way any longer.

"While I'm at the front desk making arrangements for an early-morning drive to the airport, why don't you decide where you want to go for dinner? I'll be back in a little while."

"To be honest, I'm not hungry. We had a late lunch."

"Then I'll stop at the deli for some snacks in case you change your mind later." He put on a sport shirt and left the room.

Gemma put her book down and sat on the bed, alarmed.

Vincenzo was going to renounce his title! He honestly believed that by getting rid of it, he'd be freed of the curse and Gemma would be happy. Her poor darling Vincenzo believed it would open up the way for her mother's blessing on their marriage.

But Gemma wasn't happy. Not at all.

She didn't want him to give up something that was part of him. He was already proving to be a wonderful *duca* through his vision of the *castello* and by all the great things he'd done to this point to restore the family's good name.

Unfortunately, until he could accept the whole of himself—until he could trust himself the way she trusted him—how could they be married? How could she live with herself knowing he was tearing himself and the fabric of his life apart just to be with her?

Gemma couldn't let him renounce the title, she just couldn't. She wouldn't let him. Somehow she had to find a way to stop him.

Oh, help! Her mother wasn't even home from her trip yet. She didn't know Vincenzo was back in Gemma's life! Gemma hadn't told Mirella about the job at the *castello* yet, either. She thought Gemma and Filippa were out together looking for jobs.

Propelled by anxiety, she headed to the bathroom

for a quick shower. Then she started packing, trying to sort out her thoughts. She wouldn't be able to work on Vincenzo tonight, not when he had Dimi's family on his mind. In a few days she would find the right time to beg him to listen to her, but it couldn't be right now.

As for her mother, Gemma would wait until she returned from England before she told her the news that would shake her *mamma*'s world once more.

An hour later Vincenzo returned and could see Gemma had showered. Her bags were basically packed and now she was in bed looking a beautiful golden honey blond. Though she'd opened the same book she'd been reading earlier, the page never turned.

Before they'd come on this trip, she'd claimed to be all mixed up. But these days in Greece had proved to him they were divinely happy doing the kinds of things other couples did on vacation. So why had the announcement she'd wanted to hear caused her to lose her concentration? Whatever was going on, he intended to get to the bottom of it.

She looked up at him with those dazzling green eyes. "Hi."

"*Buonasera.* I bought a few spinach rolls in case you want them."

"Thank you. Maybe I'll try one in a little while. Vincenzo? When you talk of marriage, do you even know where you'd want to live? You have a huge business empire in New York and are building one here. Once the resort is running smoothly, do you intend to go back and forth to the States? Are you and your friends going to put other people in charge at the *castello*? Don't they have to get back to New York, too?"

He unbuttoned his shirt before getting ready to shower and flashed her a piercing glance. "Don't you think I need an answer to *my* question first? The most important one I'll ever ask?"

Without waiting for a response, he went into the bathroom. When he came out later wearing his bathrobe, he discovered her, white-faced, sitting on the side of the bed in her nightgown, waiting for him.

"Vincenzo—I *can't* answer your question."

They'd been through this before. He shuddered. "Why not?"

"Because I've thought long and hard about it, and I don't want you to renounce your title. Not for me. I couldn't live with it."

"I'm not doing it for you. I thought you understood me. Isn't that what our whole trip has been about? Enjoying life like normal people?"

She got to her feet. "But you're not an ordinary man."

He shook his head. "Thank you for your nonanswer. I finally understand the meaning of déjà vu." After shutting off the lights, he climbed in his side of the bed. "I'm tired, Gemma. We have an early-morning call."

So saying, he turned away from her, unable to deal with this right now. Dimi's words were screaming in his head.

Just be warned. You've been in hell for years. Two weeks with her might still not be enough to make her see the light.

CHAPTER NINE

GEMMA HADN'T SLEPT at all and was numb with pain.
Vincenzo's rare show of sarcasm last night, followed
by his silence, was worse than any visible anger.

On Friday morning he rented a car at the airport
in Milan and drove them to an area off the Duomo
with a few secluded properties of the wealthy. She
wasn't surprised when he pulled into the courtyard
of a small, exquisite nineteenth-century palazzo. This
represented the world he intended to give up.

After what he'd told her last night, she believed
him. Her opinion *didn't* enter into his decision to give
up the title. He'd hated it all his life and didn't want
anything to do with it, period!

But in her heart she felt it was wrong, because he
was the best thing that had happened to the Gagliardi
family in two hundred years. Though she couldn't
convince him of this, maybe Dimi would listen before it was too late.

Vincenzo helped her out of the car and walked
her to the front entrance. To her surprise the double
doors opened and his black-haired cousin stood there,
almost as tall as Vincenzo. In trousers and an open-
necked white shirt, he'd turned into one of the most

attractive Italian men she'd ever seen. He too had the Gagliardi build and silver eyes, though his features were his mother's.

"Dimi!" she cried. The world stopped for a moment as a myriad of memories from their youth passed through her mind. He held out his arms and she ran into them. After he'd swung her around at least three times, she cried for him to put her down. "You look so wonderful!"

He wiped his eyes. "I swear I never thought to see you again in this life. Come with me." She felt his arm go around her shoulders. "We'll go out to the garden to talk."

"I'll look in on Zia Consolata while you two get reacquainted."

"*Perfetto*, Vincenzo."

Together they walked through a palazzo filled with treasures, leaving Vincenzo behind.

"How beautiful!" she exclaimed when they reached the sunroom that led to the outside patio. The rose beds were in full bloom. Dimi sat down beside her next to the wrought-iron table with an umbrella to shield them from the hot sun.

"Mamma loves it out here."

"Of course she does."

He hadn't lost that sweet smile. "Let me take a good look at you." His eyes played over her. "Short or long hair, you're a vision, Gemma. That's an extraordinary tan you and Vincenzo acquired in Greece. Your body was so white that day at the lake when—"

"Don't you dare say another word!"

Dimi burst into laughter. The sound took her back years. "I see my cousin told you about that."

"I'd rather not think about it." She reached over and grasped his hand. "He's told me all about your mother...and now your father."

His features sobered. "To be honest, I'm surprised his diseased liver held out as long as it did."

She squeezed his fingers before letting him go. "I understand your mother isn't aware of what has happened."

"No. Besides Alzheimer's, she has developed bradycardia, a slow heartbeat. The doctor inserted a pacemaker, but her body has rejected it. She's close to death now and never leaves her room."

"Would it be possible for me to talk to her?"

"That wouldn't be a good idea. She gets agitated by anyone who comes. But you're welcome to look in on her before you leave."

"Thank you." A lump had lodged in her throat. "Dimi, how can we help you with your father's funeral? Vincenzo couldn't get here soon enough."

"That's the way it has always been between us. If you want to know the truth, there's little to be done. My cousin and I are planning on the priest giving a blessing at the grave site tomorrow morning behind the *castello*. That's where all the Gagliardis are buried. No one will be invited."

"Not even me?" she asked in a small voice.

Gemma knew the location well. It was located in a special section deep in the forest. Vincenzo had met her there several times and had given her a history of the Gagliardi line. There was one spectacular monument among the headstones where the first Duca di Lombardi was buried. But she hadn't visited the family cemetery since coming to the *castello*. Duca Emanuele would be buried there now.

A strange sound came out of Dimi. "He doesn't deserve anyone as kind and loving as you being with us to say goodbye."

"Your father gave you life." Tears filled her eyes. "I can't imagine my youth without you. For that, I'm grateful to him. Something in his brain had been wired wrong, but look how you've turned out. You've been the greatest blessing to your mother, who has always adored you."

Dimi got out of the chair and paced for a few minutes, reminding her so much of Vincenzo when he had something painful on his mind. She stood up and walked over to him, putting her hands on his arms.

"You and Vincenzo are the greatest of all the Gagliardi men. I know, because I grew up with you for seventeen years and never saw anything but goodness in either of you."

He shook his head.

"I beg you to listen to me, Dimi. Don't let the actions of your fathers stain your lives and prevent you from doing the extraordinary things you were meant to do. You've both risen above the evil and corruption that entrapped them. Can't you see it's within your power to restore the good name you inherited?"

His features hardened, just like Vincenzo's did. It was uncanny. "That's a tall order, Gemma."

"Of course it isn't! Look at me." He lifted his eyes to her. "Vincenzo doesn't believe in destiny. He says your titles came as an accident of birth. Does that matter? You could raise the bar above everyone else. In fact, you've already started."

"What do you mean?"

"I've heard Vincenzo's partners talking. The two of you have hired dozens and dozens of local workers who've been unemployed to help restore the *castello* and grounds. Vincenzo started Nistri Technologies in southern Italy, putting over five hundred people to work. And Cosimo told me in private that you've started a huge new charity for Alzheimer's victims in honor of your *mamma*.

"You've done amazing things and opened doors only you could with your money and your positions as leaders. Please promise me you'll think about it and talk to him before he makes a mistake I can't bear for either of you to make."

He stared at her through narrowed eyes. "What happened to the girl who couldn't see past the title that divided you?"

She drew in a deep breath. "She grew up and is standing in front of you with no more blinders on. On this trip Vincenzo has shown me he can be a *duca* and the most wonderful man who ever lived, all at the same time. I'm so proud of both of you and all you've accomplished. It's made me see clearly at last. But he needs to believe it, too. You both do."

Gemma couldn't tell if she was getting through to Dimi or not. "Will you let me do something for you?"

"What would that be?"

"Stay with your *mamma* while you bury your father? It will be my way of showing my respect. She was a lovely woman and so kind to me. I realize she won't know me, but I can be in the room while you and Vincenzo do your part in the morning. In a small way it will make me feel connected again. If my mother weren't away on her trip, she'd want to be with the *principessa* at a time like this, too. Everyone loved her."

A mournful sigh escaped before Dimi drew her into his arms. He rocked her for a long time without saying anything. Suddenly Vincenzo's shadow fell over them.

"Zia Consolata is asleep. I'm going to run Gemma to her *pensione* right now, but I'll be back."

Dimi let her go. "I haven't even offered you something to eat or drink."

"We ate on the plane. See you soon."

Gemma waited for Dimi's answer, but he didn't say anything as he escorted her and Vincenzo through the palazzo to the front entrance. Dimi's eyes locked with Gemma's. "You have no idea what it meant to see you today."

"I feel the same way. *Piu tardi*, Dimi." She kissed his cheek and hurried out to the car. Vincenzo joined her for the twenty-minute drive to Sopri.

"Is Consolata as bad as Dimi said?"

"Worse. I can't see her lasting long now. We may have another funeral before long."

"Thank you for taking me with you to see him. I love him."

"That was quite a hug he gave you."

Within a few minutes Vincenzo pulled up to the *pensione* and helped her take in her bags. She stood at the door. "I told him I'd like to stay with Consolata in the morning. Will you let me know if he'd like that?"

His lips had formed a thin line. "I'll call you later after I've talked to him."

Gemma bit her lip as he walked back to the car and drove away. No sooner had she shut the door than her phone rang. Hoping he had regretted his hasty departure, she clicked on without checking the caller ID. Her heart was thudding. "Vincenzo?"

"No. It's Filippa."

The world spun for a moment and then settled back just as quickly. "It's great to hear your voice. Did you get the job?"

"No, I'm no longer in Canada. Instead of returning to Florence, I flew straight to Milan to see you. Do you mind if I come by the *castello* to talk? I've rented a car."

"I just got home from a trip with Vincenzo and am at the *pensione* alone. By all means, come!" Gemma knew in her heart Vincenzo wouldn't be by again today, and she needed her friend. "We'll eat lunch here and catch up."

"Thank you. You'll be saving my life."

"Let me give you instructions how to get here. My car will be out in front."

"I'll find you."

Half an hour later her darling friend came running to the door and they hugged.

"Come and sit down on the love seat. You're the last person I expected to see for a long time." She sat on the chair across from her friend, whose shoulders were shaking while she tried to hold back tears. "Talk to me, Filippa."

"Oh, Gemma—"

"I can't believe you didn't get the position."

"I did get it—but I was so homesick, I knew I

couldn't live there. If I'd had a chance to work in New York, I know it would have affected me the same way. All this time I thought I wanted to go to someplace new in the world and make my mark. By the time my orientation was over, I had to tell the owner I couldn't take the job."

Little did she know Gemma had told Vincenzo she couldn't accept the position. Twice, in fact! But not for the same reason.

"I felt terrible about it, but he was very nice. Do you know what's funny? He'd moved there from Hong Kong to start a new restaurant that's very successful."

That *was* funny, but Gemma didn't laugh and moved over to put an arm around her. "I'm so sorry."

"I'm okay, but I'm embarrassed to go home and tell the family their daughter who's never going to get married is a great big baby."

"No, you're not. Vincenzo and I have spent the last nine days in Paxos on a beach. If I thought I had to go there alone, beautiful as it is, and cook at a restaurant with no friends or family for thousands of miles, I couldn't do it."

"That's not true."

"I wouldn't lie about something like that."

Her brows lifted. "This trip you took. Does it mean—"

"No. We haven't been together like that. I'm not sure we ever will be now, but I'll talk to you about it later. Let's concentrate on you. You're welcome to stay with me on the couch for as long as you want."

"I wouldn't do that to you, but if you're willing to put me up for one night, I'll leave for home tomorrow."

"You've got to stay a couple of days at least. I don't have to be to work until Monday."

"You always make me feel good."

"Ditto. To be truthful, you couldn't have shown up at a better time for me. Vincenzo and I had to come home early from our vacation. His uncle died and he has to be with Dimi to plan the funeral. Come in the kitchen. I made a salad for us."

"Oh, it's so great to see you! What on earth was I thinking to go off, when the world I love is right here?"

"That's what I'm trying to convince Vincenzo of. He's planning to renounce his title, something that's part of him. I don't want him to do that, not for me nor for himself.

"Filippa—he doesn't think he's a whole man because of it. Somehow he's got to develop faith in himself that he can be a good man and a good *duca* at the same time. I couldn't marry him knowing he was giving it up partly because of me. The problem is, I've agreed to stay on at the *castello* for three months no matter what happens. I'm praying that in that amount of time he'll begin to see what I see."

They ate and later went to a movie. After they got back around nine, her phone rang. It was Vincenzo. With her hand shaking, she picked up and said hello.

"Gemma? I've been busy making arrangements for the burial and haven't talked to Dimi yet. If you haven't heard from him by now, then I would imagine he has decided against your staying with my aunt. I'll see you at the *castello* on Monday. Takis is calling a meeting."

She pressed a hand to her heart. "I'll be there." She

fought the tremor in her voice. "Thank you again for the trip of a lifetime, Vincenzo."

"I'm glad you enjoyed it. *Buonanotte.*"

Click.

Gemma made up a bed for Filippa on the couch, then pulled back the covers to get into her own bed. There'd been no life in Vincenzo's voice. Her grief had gone way beyond tears.

As she slid beneath the bedding, her phone rang again. This time the caller ID reflected an unknown number. She answered it with a frown. "*Pronto?*"

"Gemma? It's Dimi." She couldn't believe it. "I've decided I would like you to be here with Mamma while I'm gone. I called the *castello* for your address and phone number." *Not Vincenzo?* "I'll be by for you at eight o'clock in the morning."

Joy. "I'm honored and I'll be ready."

After she got off the phone, she ran into the living room and told Filippa. "I want you to stay. I won't be gone for more than a couple of hours."

"All right."

Like the night before, Gemma didn't get much sleep. The next morning she showered early and put on the one black dress she had in her wardrobe. It had capped sleeves and a slim skirt. Nothing fancy, but she felt it was appropriate.

Her friend had gotten busy in the kitchen and fixed them a delicious breakfast. When Dimi came for her, she didn't know who looked more surprised, him or Filippa.

It was very interesting to feel the aura that surrounded two stunned, beautiful people before Gemma introduced them. Dimi wore a black mourning suit. Filippa had put on a summer dress in a small blue-and-white print, bringing out the intensity of her blue eyes.

When Gemma explained why Filippa was there, he turned to her friend. "Please come with us so Gemma doesn't have to sit alone."

"I don't want to intrude in such a private matter."

"You're her best friend. We have no secrets and it's no intrusion. If you're ready, let's go."

They walked out to the black limousine with the insignia and coat of arms of the Duca di Lombardi. When they got in the back, Dimi placed himself across from them with his long legs crossed at the ankles. All the way to the palazzo, Gemma sat there in wonder as he and Filippa talked quietly, sharing small confidences so naturally, it surprised her.

By the time they reached their destination, Gemma was convinced something of consequence was happening between them. Dimi's eyes never left her face. As for Filippa, her expression had to have mimicked Gemma's the first time she'd seen the dashing, grown-up Vincenzo in the office at the *castello*. If any man ran a close second to Vincenzo, it was his cousin.

He led them inside his mother's bedroom. A health care worker sat beside the bed. Dimi showed the two of them to comfortable upholstered chairs in a corner of the room. He made arrangements for food and drinks to be brought to the small table if they wanted them.

Gemma squeezed his hand. "God bless you today, Dimi."

He kissed her cheek. "Thank you for doing this."

His eyes swerved to Filippa. The look he gave her friend was a revelation. "Thank you for coming with her. I won't be long."

A cloudy sky above the opening in the forest didn't allow the sunlight to shine on the casket. Vincenzo and Dimi stood side by side holding long-stemmed yellow roses while Father Janos delivered the funeral prayer.

"Here we have gathered in memory of Alonzo Trussardi Gagliardi, second in line to the Duca di Lombardi, so that we may together perform one final duty of love. As an act of remembrance, we have gathered to place his remains here in this sacred resting spot. In so doing, we trust that somehow what was best in his life will not be lost, but will rejoin the great web of creation.

"May the truth that sets us free, and the hope that never dies, and the love that casts out fear be with us now until dayspring breaks and the shadows flee away. We have been blessed by life—go in peace. Amen." He made the sign of the cross.

Dimi placed his rose on the casket, then Vincenzo. They both thanked the priest and had just started to walk away when Dimi said, "Let's go over to your father's grave before we drive back to the palazzo." He pulled two more long-stemmed roses from a planter vase for them.

Vincenzo hadn't visited it since he'd been back in Italy. He hadn't ever planned to take a last look, but something fundamental had changed in him since he'd been with Gemma. All their long talks about the past had forced him to delve deep inside himself for the first time in ten years. Perhaps it was time.

His father's grave was behind a nearby tree. They looked at the writing on the headstone. Was it possible that all the evil had been buried with him and hadn't been handed down to Vincenzo? He wanted to believe it. He wanted to believe Gemma, whose soul had been in her eyes when she'd begged him to keep the title and do great things with it. If he thought he could…

Dimi turned to him. "Gemma gave me a piece of advice earlier."

Gemma again, Vincenzo mused. She'd had a profound effect on both of them.

"She said not to let our fathers' misdeeds stain our lives. Though my father was never the *duca*, he'd always hoped to be one day. But no matter what, being the offspring of the old duca didn't make him or your father who they were. It was a flaw in them. She was right, you know?"

With those words he placed his rose at the base of the stone. Clearly Dimi had forgiven both their fathers.

Gemma had forgiven them, too. She'd seen the example of the old *duca* and she believed in Vincenzo. That belief caused an epiphany in him.

As he stood there, he realized his faith in himself had been restored. Stunned and humbled, he put his own rose by the headstone. Then they walked back to the limousine. Vincenzo had come to the cemetery in his car parked behind the limo.

"I'll follow you to the palazzo, Dimi. I don't want you to be alone today."

His cousin eyed him oddly. "I won't be. Gemma

and her friend are there. I picked them up early this morning so they could sit with Mamma."

Vincenzo reeled from the news. "What friend?"

"Filippa. I'm sure she's told you about her."

"Yes, but I thought she was in Canada interviewing for a pastry chef position."

"It seems it didn't work out and she came back last evening."

"A lot has gone on since I dropped Gemma off yesterday."

Dimi nodded. "I told you we talked while you were with Mamma. Something she said, plus what Father Janos said today, has decided me against renouncing the title."

Vincenzo knew the line he was talking about. It had struck a chord with Vincenzo, too.

"Remember the part, 'We trust that somehow what was best in his life will not be lost, but will rejoin the great web of creation'? Gemma convinced me there's a lot you and I can do if we keep our titles to create something really good to repair the damage. In my soul I know she's right." He opened the rear door. "I'll see you back at the palazzo, cousin."

Vincenzo stood there for a few minutes pondering everything. Little did Dimi know he'd been preaching to the converted. In time he broke free of his thoughts long enough to jump in his car. He took off behind Dimi, intending to talk to Gemma as soon as possible.

Dimi was waiting for him in the courtyard when he pulled in. "Have you ever met Gemma's friend?" Dimi asked as they went inside.

Vincenzo hadn't expected that question. His cousin's decision not to renounce his title had been superseded by something else—like the fact that Dimi had a woman on his mind when they'd just laid his uncle to rest.

"Not yet."

Once they entered the palazzo, he followed him through the house to his aunt's bedroom. There he found Gemma and her friend talking quietly to one of the health care workers.

The older woman said Consolata had been resting comfortably all morning, which was a relief. Vincenzo tore his gaze from a pair of green eyes to a pair of blue ones. He had to agree with Gemma's assessment—with that coloring, Filippa was a knockout. Dimi told them to come to the sunroom. When they stood up, he noticed Signorina Gatti was a little shorter than Gemma, but just as curvaceous.

Outside in the garden, formal introductions were made. The maid served them iced tea and sandwiches. Dimi wasn't inclined to talk about the funeral service. If anything he seemed intrigued by Filippa and asked her about her trip to Canada.

Vincenzo took advantage of the moment to get Gemma alone. "We need to talk. How long is your friend going to be with you?"

"She's driving back to Florence tomorrow."

"I'll take the two of you to your place as soon as you're ready to leave. Hopefully we'll find time to be alone tomorrow after she's gone."

Before he could hear her answer, Dimi had walked over. "I've told Filippa I'd like to drive her back to the *pensione* later. What are your plans?"

This day wasn't going the way Vincenzo had imagined at all. He'd thought he might be able to console his cousin, but it didn't look like he needed it. Under the circumstances, nothing could have suited Vincenzo better than to get Gemma alone without offending her friend. He had something vital to tell her.

Gemma gave Filippa the key to the *pensione.* They all said goodbye and Vincenzo walked out to his car with Gemma. But when they left the heart of the city, he turned onto the A8 motorway.

Her head jerked around. "Where are we going? This isn't the way to Sopri."

"First you need to answer a question for me. What magic did you weave on Dimi that has caused him to want to keep his title? He has spent a lifetime telling me he despised it."

"I'm glad he feels that way." She sounded overjoyed.

He gripped the steering wheel tighter. "Was that your plan? To get him on your side so he'd try to influence me?"

"I'd do *anything* to get you on my side! I've finally realized why you don't want to keep the title. You think you can't be a whole person unless you renounce that part that has pained you. But don't you see? You've already done so many things for the community, for your country since you've come back. You're an extraordinary man by being exactly who you are. I don't want you diminished in any way, shape or form. I love you, Vincenzo, title and all."

He didn't know where to go with his emotions. It seemed he didn't have to explain how his feelings had changed about the title and the good he could do with it. "I'm glad you feel that way, because I've de-

cided to keep it. Does that mean you'll marry me?"
This was the last time he was going to ask.

"Yes, yes, *yes!*"

CHAPTER TEN

JOY ROCKED VINCENZO'S WORLD, but he groaned aloud. "*Gemma*—what a time to tell me! I'm driving and can't pull over right now. The summer traffic will be bumper to bumper like this all the way to Lake Como."

"That's where we're going?"

"If we can ever get there. Everyone's trying to leave Milan at the same time."

An infectious giggle came out of her, a happy sound he hadn't heard in years. "We've practiced self-control for the last few weeks. Another hour won't kill us."

"You mean *two*. It's *killing* me, you beautiful witch." He reached for her hand and clung to it.

"I want to marry you, Vincenzo. I'm crazy, madly, terrifyingly in love with you. I'm sorry it's taken me so long to get my head on straight. Please—while you can't touch me and I can't make love to you—tell me where we're going to live. I want to know everything. Will we fly back and forth from here to New York every few months? The suspense is killing me."

"One answer at a time. We're going to live here permanently."

"You really mean it?" That was pure happiness he heard in her voice. "Where is here, exactly?"

"That's what I want to show you."

"You mean at Lake Como?"

"The first night in Greece, when we were on the beach, you said that to live surrounded by water would be paradise. I've always wanted to live by water, too. There's a place I've had my eye on for the last six months, never dreaming I'd find you again. And it's not too far from the *castello*."

"I've never been to Lake Como. Have you already bought it?"

"No. The Realtor has been holding it for me, but my time is almost up."

"What town is it in?"

"Cernobbio, in the foothills of the Alps, where the scenery truly is magnificent."

"Is it as fantastic as I'm imagining it is?"

"You'll have to wait and see. I'm sure your mother will love it. She'll be living with us, wherever we are. When the traffic is light, it's only a little over an hour's drive from Milan. There's a private dock on the lake, so we'll have to buy a boat."

"She doesn't know about us yet."

"I didn't think she did. When will she be back from her trip?"

"Tomorrow."

"That's perfect. We'll drive to Florence tomorrow and tell her we're getting married. She loves you enough to want what you want. I'll spend the rest of my life proving to her our marriage will work. But the ceremony has to happen before the grand opening, so we only have a few days left to plan it."

"I'm so happy, I feel like I'm going burst!"

"Don't do that while we're still in this traffic."

She grabbed onto his arm. "When we're married, if the traffic is too horrible to drive home, we can always go upstairs to the tower room, and we'll hibernate while I feed you *sfogliatelli*. No one will know where we are."

Vincenzo didn't know how much longer he could last without pulling Gemma onto his lap. "The one thing we won't have at Lake Como is a beach. Almost no property has beachfront."

"There's only one beach I want. It's in Greece. You've spoiled me. I know I'm dreaming. Do you care if I keep working?"

"I want you to be happy, whatever it takes."

"Will you be happy living away from New York?"

"I have a confession to make. I was never happy there."

"Honestly?"

"I'm an Italian. I was homesick."

Gemma let out a cry. "Filippa said the same thing. That's why she's back."

"Good for her. Where would you like to get married, *bellissima*?"

"I think that should be up to you."

"Then I say we ask the priest to marry us in the *castello* chapel."

"That would make me the happiest woman on earth." Tears ran down her tanned cheeks. "It is so beautiful. I remember looking inside when your grandfather was in there. I thought it was the closest place to heaven."

"Have you considered what he was trying to tell

you that day out in the courtyard might have had a different meaning? My belief is that he knew you were my soul's delight and saw you as the princess I would marry one day."

"Do you really think that?"

"Yes. I'm going to tell your mother that. She'll have to be happy for us."

Gemma's eyes filled with tears. "I'll treasure what you've said all my life."

"You're *my* treasure, Gemma."

"Oh, I can't wait until we get there."

Another few minutes and they passed through Como. Cernobbio was only a little farther up the lake. When they reached it, Gemma gasped. "I didn't know scenery like this existed on earth. There are dozens of incredible villas!"

He wound around until they came to one that jutted out into the lake. At the sign—Villa Gagliardi—he slowed to a stop on the private road.

Gemma took it in with disbelieving eyes before she turned to Vincenzo. "This villa belonged to your family?"

He nodded. "Until my father gambled it away. I've negotiated to buy it back. It's ours if you want it."

"If I *want* it?" She launched herself at him, throwing her arms around his bronzed neck. "I want you forever, any way I can have you. I'll take anything that comes with you."

For the next little while, they tried without success to show each other how much they loved and wanted each other. It was impossible within the confines of his Maserati.

"How can you do this to me?" he whispered against

her lips. "For nine days you held me off. Now you're giving yourself to me and I can't do a thing about it until we find a place to be alone."

"I know. I'm sorry, but I promise I'll make it up to you."

"Let's get married the day after tomorrow. No man ever needed a wedding night more than I do."

She buried her face in his neck. "How can we do that? Wouldn't you have to get a special license?"

"Yes. But I'm the Duca di Lombardi. I'm the person who makes these things happen." His smile melted her bones.

"I presume Father Janos will perform the ceremony whenever you say."

He nodded.

"Won't he think it's too soon after the funeral?"

"Not at all. He'll be happy we're making a dream come true in the midst of so much sadness."

She kissed every feature of his face. "Is there anything you can't do?"

"No."

"Vincenzo—" She hugged him harder. "Be serious. You want to get married the day after tomorrow?"

"Don't you? With your mother coming back tomorrow, there's no reason to delay it a second longer."

"I love you, *il mio amore.*"

"Then we need to drive back to Milan immediately and make all the arrangements. Besides your mother, I want Dimi and my partners there."

"I'll tell Filippa she can't leave for Florence until after the ceremony. She can stay at the *pensione* until then."

"Kiss me one more time, Gemma, so I know I'm not hallucinating."

"I plan to kiss the daylights out of you after we say 'I do.' But since I shouldn't be bothering you while you're driving, I'm going to call Mamma right now and tell her everything. She can think about it on her flight back to Florence."

He squeezed her arm. "I'll talk to her, too, and tell her we've just come from the home where we want her to live with us."

Gemma was euphoric as she pulled out her phone to reach her mother. No matter her parent's first reaction, Gemma would talk her down, because there was no one like Vincenzo. She planned to be his wife, and her mother had to understand that.

The phone rang a few times until Mirella picked up. "Oh, Gemma—I'm so glad it's you. I'm tired of traveling around and am anxious to come home."

"I can't wait for you to get here, but please don't be too tired, Mamma."

"Ah? What's wrong?"

"Everything is so right, I don't know where to start."

"You must have gotten a wonderful job."

"Oh, I did!"

After a pause, her mother said, "I haven't heard you this happy since…"

"Since we once lived at the *castello*?" she answered for her.

"Gemma? What's going on?"

"Vincenzo is back in my life! That's what's going on." She smiled into his eyes of molten silver. "You're not going to believe why he really disappeared or why he's back now. We're going to be married the day after tomorrow."

"But he's a *duca*!"

She smiled at Vincenzo through her happy tears. "Yes, and I'm going to be his *duchessa*. That's why you can't be too tired. Tomorrow we have to buy me a wedding dress and a beautiful dress for you. Filippa will need one, too. The ceremony is going to take place in the *castello* chapel by Father Janos. You remember him?"

"Lentamente, mia bambina—"

"I'm too excited to slow down. Tomorrow I'll tell you all the details while we're looking for dresses."

Vincenzo took the phone from her. "Mirella? We want your blessing. No one knows better than you how much I love your daughter. The day you made that little lemon ricotta cheesecake for me when I was eight was the day I fell in love with you, too. Here's Gemma back."

Tears were rolling down her cheeks as she took the phone from him. "Mamma? Did you hear what Vincenzo said?"

"I did," she answered in a croaky voice. "Tell him that if I hadn't loved him, too, I wouldn't have made it for him."

Gemma could hardly breathe. "I'll tell him. I love you, Mamma. See you tomorrow. Fly home safe."

The minute she heard the click, she told him what her mother had said. His eyes filled with tears before she broke down sobbing for joy.

When Dimi arrived at the *pensione* in the ducal limousine at three o'clock, Gemma walked outside with

Filippa, leaving the place in a complete mess. She wore the white wedding dress her mother and her friend had helped her pick out in one of the shops in Milan earlier that morning.

The skirt was a filmy chiffon that fell from the waist and floated around her legs. Lace made up the bodice and short sleeves. Instead of a veil or a bouquet, she wore a garland of white roses and a single strand of pearls with matching earrings that had been delivered that morning by courier. Vincenzo's prewedding gift.

Filippa had helped her put them on and handed her the enclosed card.

Ti amo, squisita.
You are my treasure.

The little makeup she wore was ruined by her tears, and she had to rush to repair the damage.

Gemma had wanted a simple wedding outfit that would still look bridal. If they'd been getting married in front of several hundred people, she would have chosen a long dress with a train and veil. But she was happy with their perfect little wedding.

Dimi took pictures with his camera first. Gemma insisted on taking some of him. Within minutes he helped her into the back of the limousine, where her mother was waiting in an ivory lace suit and pearls. Then he assisted Filippa.

He looked marvelous in a dark blue suit with a white rose in the lapel. Her friend wore a pale pink silk sheath with a corsage of pink roses and looked stunning.

As the limousine drove away, Gemma looked across at Dimi. She squeezed her mother's hand. "I've been thinking back through the years when we were just little children."

"Now you're all grown up." Mirella smiled at them.

"I can't believe this is really happening, Mamma."

Dimi grinned. "Neither can my cousin. He's been waiting for this day for so long, I hope he's still holding it together. I told his friends to do whatever was necessary to help him make it through to the four o'clock ceremony. It's your fault he's in this state, Gemma."

"I've been in a state since I applied for a job at the *castello*, battling my old demons."

"Vincenzo and I know all about those. But yours are gone, right?"

Filippa spoke for her. "I can promise you that my dear Gemma is the most divinely happy woman on the planet. I ought to know. For the last nine years I've listened to her pain over losing Vincenzo."

"Oh—" Mirella threw her hands in the air. "I prayed every night the pain would stop."

Gemma's friend chuckled. "The minute I heard he was alive and back at the *castello*, I actually sent up a special prayer of thanksgiving."

Dimi nodded. "I did the same thing when he told me you'd applied for the pastry chef position. It was your recipes, Mirella, that put Gemma over the top with Vincenzo's partners. Do you know that from the moment he arrived in New York, I've heard nothing but grief from him where Gemma was concerned?

Today I'm the happiest man on the planet to know that this torturefest is about to be over."

The four of them laughed.

"I love Vincenzo so much. When he walked in the office, I almost fainted."

Dimi leaned forward and patted her hand. "When you two met, we couldn't have been more than four or five. Even then it was as if no one else existed. He followed you around like a puppy dog. You teased him and provoked him, but he just kept coming."

"He teased me back constantly. His growls were terrifying when he chased me around the old ruins. I laughed until I fell down and couldn't catch my breath. Every day when I woke up, I knew I was going to see him and there'd be a new adventure. Nothing else mattered.

"But I want you to know something, Dimi. I loved you, too. So did Bianca. I don't think there were four happier children anywhere."

"I agree. What I want to know is, are you ready to be chased around the *castello*'s secret corridors and chambers for the rest of your life?"

"Yes. I can't wait!"

"Gemma!" Mirella cried, but she knew her mother was only pretending to be shocked.

"I'm warning you. He hasn't outgrown certain tendencies." His wicked smile reminded her of the old Dimi.

"Neither have I, but don't you dare tell him."

When she looked out the tinted windows, she realized the limousine had pulled up in front of the *castello* steps. She gripped her mother's hand. "This is it."

Dimi got out and held the door open for the three of them. "Be sure you want to go inside, Gemma," he teased. "Because when you do, you'll never be the same again."

"I know." She gave him a hug. "I'll be Signora Gagliardi. Don't have a heart attack, Mamma."

Her mother only laughed, the most wonderful sound Gemma had ever heard from her parent. eh.

"Well, here goes!" She took off alone and rushed up the steps, breathless to find Vincenzo, who was inside waiting for her. Never had there been a bride as eager as she to seal her fate.

Cesare stood at the entrance in a becoming tan suit. He too wore a white rose in his lapel. "Your husband-to-be has asked me to do the honors and escort you to the chapel." He kissed her on both cheeks.

"Thank you so much."

He gave her his arm and they walked through several long corridors to reach that part of the *castello*. "I had no idea when I interviewed you that you were the person who ruined every woman for Vincenzo all those years ago."

"That's not quite true. I know of one special woman, very recently in fact."

He shook his head. "No, no. If she'd been the one, he would have brought her with him. Did you know he wanted you to stay in the tower room of the former *principessa*?"

Warmth traveled up her neck to her cheeks. That had been her favorite room in the whole *castello*. "He was only joking."

Cesare laughed. "Denial becomes you."

They reached the closed chapel doors, where Takis

stood, dressed in a beige suit, also wearing a white rose. He hugged her before Dimi introduced Filippa and Gemma's mother to the other men.

Cesare gave her a special smile. "So you're the *mamma* responsible for raising our new executive pastry chef. She gave all the credit to you on her résumé. I understand why. The pastry she made for us was beyond compare. I'm honored to meet you." So saying, he gave her a kiss on both cheeks. Gemma loved him for showing her mother such deference.

Dimi turned to Filippa. "This is where I leave you to join Vincenzo, but Takis will take good care of you." Dimi's gaze swerved to Gemma's. "You're sure you want to go through with this?"

"*Dimi—*" she cried softly in exasperation.

"Just checking."

He took more pictures of all of them, then folded her mother's arm over his and they moved inside the chapel.

Gemma looked at Takis. "Have you seen Vincenzo? Is he in there?"

"*Si.*"

"And Father Janos?"

"*Si.*" With a poker face, he added, "In case you can't tell them apart, Vincenzo is the tall guy wearing the gray suit and white rose. The short, portly father is wearing...well...let's just say he's dressed in splendid robes for this once-in-a-lifetime celebration of your marriage."

Her eyes smarted. "Thank you for being his dear friends. Your friendship saved him at the darkest moment of his life."

Takis cocked his head. "Someday we'll tell you

just how dark our lives were when we arrived in the States. Meeting Vincenzo was the best thing that ever happened to us. Isn't that right, Cesare?"

The Sicilian nodded and lent her his arm. "It's four o'clock. Time to begin."

Takis opened the doors and walked Filippa down the aisle. Gemma followed with Cesare. For such a small chapel, the interior was breathtaking, with wall and ceiling frescoes still vibrant with color.

This was where she'd seen Vincenzo's grandfather worship. Now Emanuele's two grandsons stood on either side of Father Janos, waiting for Gemma. She feared her heartbeat could be heard throughout the incense-sweet interior. With each step that took her closer to Vincenzo, it seemed to grow louder.

Except for the absence of the father she'd never known, Gemma couldn't imagine a more perfect setting for their intimate wedding. The most important people in the world were here in attendance.

Cesare walked her to the front, where Vincenzo reached for her hands. Beneath his black wavy hair, the bronzed features of his striking face stood out against the frescoes. The candles beneath the shrine cast flickering shadows, revealing to Gemma the impossibility of his male beauty.

They both whispered, "*Ti amo...*" at the same time.

Father Janos bestowed a thoughtful smile on them. "I understand this moment has been in the making for many years."

She nodded. Vincenzo must have told him everything.

"That is a good long time for you to have loved each other and should give you the faith that your union will be blessed by the Almighty. Vincenzo? Take her right hand in your left and repeat after me. 'I, Vincenzo Nistri Gagliardi, Duca di Lombardi, take Gemma Bonucci Rizzo for my beloved wife. I will love her, cherish her, protect her for the rest of my life.'"

Gemma heard him repeat the words in that deep, thrilling voice of his.

"Now, Gemma. Repeat these words."

She looked into Vincenzo's eyes. Between the dark lashes they gleamed pure silver. "I, Gemma Bonucci Rizzo, take Vincenzo Nistri Gagliardi, Duca de Lombardi, for my beloved husband, who has always been beloved to me." The last part of the sentence was her own addition. It brought a smile to Vincenzo's lips.

"I will love him, cherish him, support him and honor him for the rest of my life." The honor part was another deviation from the script, but she wanted him to know how complete was her commitment to him.

"Because you have taken these vows, I pronounce you man and wife. In the name of the Father, the Son and the Holy Spirit. Amen. Vincenzo? Do you have a ring?"

"I do."

"You may present it to your wife.

She was his wife!

His fingers were sure as he pushed home a diamond in a gold band on her ring finger.

"Do you have a ring, Gemma?"

"She does," Dimi said and came forward. He handed her the gold band she'd picked out for Vincenzo during their shopping spree with her mother.

"You may present it to your husband."

Vincenzo helped her put it on, then pulled her into his arms and kissed her. It went on for a long, long time. Gemma forgot everything and everyone. Somehow she'd been given her heart's desire, and nothing mattered but to pledge her heart and soul to him in the most intimate way she knew how.

"I love you, Gemma. You just don't know how much."

"But I do, *amore mio.*"

They kissed each other once more. When he finally lifted his mouth from hers, she realized they were the only ones left in the chapel. "Oh, no—even the priest has gone."

He gave her that white smile to die for. "Father Janos was a man before he wore the robes. That should answer your question."

"There's no one like you. It was a perfect wedding."

Vincenzo wrapped his arms around her. "There's more. Much as I want to take you upstairs, our friends are waiting in my grandfather's small dining room to celebrate with us. I'm excited, because Cesare's contribution has been to make the meal for us. He learned to cook from his mother, just the way you did. It'll be an all-Sicilian menu tonight."

She put her arms around his neck. "I love your friends. I adore Dimi, and I love my dear friend Filippa. I've decided her timing in coming back to Italy was meant to be, as was Mamma's. Now I guess we'd better not keep them all waiting."

He kissed her eyes, nose and mouth. "They understand and will enjoy the vintage Sicilian wine until we get there. One more kiss, *sposa mia.*"

Twenty minutes later they walked arm in arm to the second floor. When they entered the dining room, Gemma could smell the beef fillet in brandy before she saw the paintings of wood nymphs, all in a serious state of undress. Her face turned scarlet.

Everyone clapped. Vincenzo walked her to the table and sat down next to her, putting his hand on her thigh beneath the table. Heat coursed through her body.

Dimi raised his glass. "To my cousin and his wife. To Mirella. None of you have any idea how long I've wanted to say that. I don't know when I've ever been this happy." His eyes were smiling. So were Filippa's.

Cosimo waited on them, bringing one delicious dish after another. Caponata...*arancini*...pasta with urchin sauce.

When the meal concluded, Gemma got to her feet. "This is joy beyond measure to be surrounded by our friends and my beloved mother. What can I say about our bridal feast? The six-star award goes to Cesare for the best meal I've ever eaten in my life. *Grazie* with all my heart."

Cesare beamed. "*Di niente.*"

Vincenzo stood up and put his arm around Gemma's waist. "I can't improve on anything my bride said. And now I must tell you we have a pressing engagement elsewhere and ask to be excused, but we know you will understand."

The men's deep laughter filled the room while Filippa and Gemma exchanged a secret smile. With her friend planning to stay at the *pensione* for a few more days, everything was working out perfectly. On a whim, Gemma removed her garland of roses and tossed it to Filippa, then tossed her mother a kiss. She would be staying in the tower room of the *principessa* until after the hotel's grand opening. Vincenzo couldn't do enough for her.

"Come with me," her husband whispered.

She needed no urging. Her desire for him had reached a flashpoint.

Vincenzo rushed her through the hallways to the back of the *castello*. When they came to the winding steps, he picked her up in his arms and carried her to the tower room. His strength astounded her. When they'd reached the bedroom, he wasn't even out of breath.

"I've dreamed of doing that for years. Help me, Gemma. I want you so much I'm shaking."

While he was helping her out of her dress, she was trying to take off his suit jacket. Somehow they managed and kissed their way to the bed. He lay down with her and crushed her in his arms, entwining his legs with hers. After suppressing their needs for the last two weeks, the freedom to love each other made her delirious with longing.

Each touch and caress ignited their passion. Vincenzo had lit her on fire. The right to show her husband everything she felt and wanted was a heady experience too marvelous to contain. They drank deeply from each other's mouths, thrilling in the wonder of being together like this.

Far into the night, they gave and took pleasure with no thought but the happiness and joy they found in each other. Gemma hadn't known the physical side of their lovemaking could be this overwhelming. Her rapture was so great that at times she cried afterward and clung to him.

When morning came he began the age-old ritual all over again. They'd suffered for so long, they thoroughly enjoyed becoming one flesh, one heart.

Toward noon, they lay side by side, awake again. Vincenzo smiled at her. "I feel like I've just been reborn."

"I know. I've had those same feelings."

He suddenly pulled her on top of him. "I'm too happy, Gemma."

"Can there be too much happiness?"

"I don't know. Promise me it will always be like this."

She searched his eyes. "My love for you just keeps growing."

Rolling her over, he kissed her fiercely. "I want to make love to you all over again, but I know you must be hungry. Are you?"

"Yes. For you!"

"I'm serious."

"So am I."

"Cesare told me yesterday he'd have food brought up to us. I'm pretty sure it's outside the door now."

"Then we'd better eat it. I don't want to hurt his feelings." Her darling Vincenzo. He was starving, but he didn't want to admit it. She loved this man beyond description. "Why don't you go look and see?"

He pressed a kiss to her throat. "I'll be right back. Don't go away."

"Where would I go?"

"Never disappear on me, Gemma. I couldn't take it." Lines had darkened his face.

She couldn't understand it and pulled him back. "Someone once said, 'Don't give in to your fears. If you do, you won't be able to talk to your heart.'"

"That was Paulo Coelho."

Gemma caught his handsome face in her hands. "You're disgustingly intelligent, my love, but you need to take his advice. Don't you know I plan to cling to you forever?"

"I'm besotted with you, Gemma." He hurried to the door in his robe and came back with a tray of food that smelled divine. "Cesare has really outdone himself."

She took it from him and put it on the bed. "Let's eat fast so I can love you all over again."

His smile melted her bones. "I'm planning to keep you locked up here forever."

She leaned across to kiss his jaw. He needed a shave. "That's fine as long as you let me out in time for the grand opening. It'll be here in a few days. I was hired to cook, remember?"

Those silvery eyes blazed with fire for her. "Do you think I can ever forget anything since you came back into my life?"

He ate his cheese-and-ham strata in record time, displaying the appetite she always associated with him. Then he put the tray on the floor. After taking her in his arms again, he buried his face in her neck.

"We were meant to be together from the beginning. Love me, *sposa squisita*. I was hooked from the first time I saw the cutest little honey-blonde girl on earth come running out to the ruins to play hide and go seek. Her eyes were greener than the grass and her smile was like sunshine. My five-year-old heart quivered, and that has never changed."

"*Vincenzo*—"

EPILOGUE

THE MORNING OF the day before the grand opening, Gemma worked with her team as they prepared everything. While she was supervising the tiramisu desserts, Cesare walked in the kitchen and came over to her.

"*Per favore*, will you stop what you're doing and come out in the hall? This will only take a minute."

"Of course." She washed her hands and wiped them on her apron as she hurried after him. Once through the doors she came to a full stop. *Paolo!*

Cesare said, "I understand you two know each other."

"Yes. It's good to see you, Paolo."

He gave her a slight nod. "I understand you're Signora Gagliardi now. I get why it didn't work out for us. The Duca di Lombardi was the man you could never forget."

"You're right."

"Congratulations on your marriage."

"Thank you."

"*Buon Appetito* magazine has sent me out to cover the grand opening of the restaurant tomorrow and write up my opinion. Knowing that *you're* the new executive pastry chef has blown me away. Signor Donati told me I could say hello to you if I waited out here. I realize how busy you must be, so I won't keep you. *Buona fortuna*, Gemma."

She felt his sincerity, though that didn't mean he wouldn't be brutal if her food didn't measure up to his idea of five-star dining. "To you, too, Paolo. *Grazie*."

Two mornings later

While Gemma lay wrapped in her husband's arms, both still exhausted from all the work of the grand opening, she heard a knock.

"Vincenzo, get up and see what I've slipped under your door."

At the sound of Cesare's voice, both of them came awake. *The reviews!*

"*Grazie!*"

"Stay there, *caro*." Gemma bounded out of bed first and grabbed her husband's robe to put on. Half a dozen computer printouts had been pushed through. She reached for them and ran back to the bed.

By now Vincenzo was fully awake. He threw his arm around her shoulders while they read the glowing reviews. Then his cell phone rang. He saw the caller ID and picked up, holding the phone so Gemma could hear, too.

"Dimi?"

"Have you read everything yet?" His cousin sounded ecstatic.

"Almost."

"Our cup has run over today."

"I agree."

"I'm bringing Filippa to the *castello* with me later on today and we'll celebrate."

"That sounds perfect. Ciao."

He hung up and they began to read Paolo's article.

A new star is born in Lombardi!

Ring out the bells for the Castello Supremo Hotel and Ristorante di Lombardi. From its hundred-years-old ducal past has emerged a triumph of divine ambience and cuisine so exquisite to the palate, this critic can't find enough superlatives. One could live forever on the slow-cooked boeuf bourguignon and the *sfogliatelli* Mirella dessert alone. This critic thought he'd died and gone to heaven.

It deserves six stars. Bravo!

Gemma put it down and threw her arms around Vincenzo's neck. "You and Dimi and your partners did it, *amante*! You did it!" She broke down crying for joy.

"We all did it, including your wonderful *mamma*."

"Was it your idea to name the dessert after her?"

He studied her features before kissing her passionately. "It was Cesare's. An Italian loves his mother. After hearing your story, he knew your *mamma* deserved the credit on the souvenir menu commemorating the opening."

"That's so sweet of him. When Mamma sees this, she'll die."

"I have a better idea. Let's frame it, along with a menu, and give them to her for a special present. Cesare was touched that you loved your mother so much you talked about her on your application. I already know how sweet you are.

"The day you came running outside with the lemon ricotta cheesecake she made for my birthday, you ran straight into my heart and never left. You'll always be there. *Ti amo*, Signora Gagliardi."

"*Ti amo*, Your Highness."

"Don't call me that."

"It's the highest honor I can give you, Vincenzo. You're the greatest Gagliardi of them all."

* * * * *

Look out for two more stories in
The Billionaire's Club coming soon!

You might also enjoy Rebecca Winters'
MONTINARI MARRIAGES *Trilogy*

THE BILLIONAIRE'S BABY SWAP
THE BILLIONAIRE WHO SAW HER BEAUTY
THE BILLIONAIRE'S PRIZE

MILLS & BOON®
Hardback – March 2017

ROMANCE

Secrets of a Billionaire's Mistress	Sharon Kendrick
Claimed for the De Carrillo Twins	Abby Green
The Innocent's Secret Baby	Carol Marinelli
The Temporary Mrs Marchetti	Melanie Milburne
A Debt Paid in the Marriage Bed	Jennifer Hayward
The Sicilian's Defiant Virgin	Susan Stephens
Pursued by the Desert Prince	Dani Collins
The Forgotten Gallo Bride	Natalie Anderson
Return of Her Italian Duke	Rebecca Winters
The Millionaire's Royal Rescue	Jennifer Faye
Proposal for the Wedding Planner	Sophie Pembroke
A Bride for the Brooding Boss	Bella Bucannon
Their Secret Royal Baby	Carol Marinelli
Her Hot Highland Doc	Annie O'Neil
His Pregnant Royal Bride	Amy Ruttan
Baby Surprise for the Doctor Prince	Robin Gianna
Resisting Her Army Doc Rival	Susan MacKay
A Month to Marry the Midwife	Fiona McArthur
Billionaire's Baby Promise	Sarah M. Anderson
Seduce Me, Cowboy	Maisey Yates

MILLS & BOON®
Large Print – March 2017

ROMANCE

Di Sione's Virgin Mistress	Sharon Kendrick
Snowbound with His Innocent Temptation	Cathy Williams
The Italian's Christmas Child	Lynne Graham
A Diamond for Del Rio's Housekeeper	Susan Stephens
Claiming His Christmas Consequence	Michelle Smart
One Night with Gael	Maya Blake
Married for the Italian's Heir	Rachael Thomas
Christmas Baby for the Princess	Barbara Wallace
Greek Tycoon's Mistletoe Proposal	Kandy Shepherd
The Billionaire's Prize	Rebecca Winters
The Earl's Snow-Kissed Proposal	Nina Milne

HISTORICAL

The Runaway Governess	Liz Tyner
The Winterley Scandal	Elizabeth Beacon
The Queen's Christmas Summons	Amanda McCabe
The Discerning Gentleman's Guide	Virginia Heath

MEDICAL

A Daddy for Her Daughter	Tina Beckett
Reunited with His Runaway Bride	Robin Gianna
Rescued by Dr Rafe	Annie Claydon
Saved by the Single Dad	Annie Claydon
Sizzling Nights with Dr Off-Limits	Janice Lynn
Seven Nights with Her Ex	Louisa Heaton

MILLS & BOON®
Hardback – April 2017

ROMANCE

The Italian's One-Night Baby	Lynne Graham
The Desert King's Captive Bride	Annie West
Once a Moretti Wife	Michelle Smart
The Boss's Nine-Month Negotiation	Maya Blake
The Secret Heir of Alazar	Kate Hewitt
Crowned for the Drakon Legacy	Tara Pammi
His Mistress with Two Secrets	Dani Collins
The Argentinian's Virgin Conquest	Bella Frances
Stranded with the Secret Billionaire	Marion Lennox
Reunited by a Baby Bombshell	Barbara Hannay
The Spanish Tycoon's Takeover	Michelle Douglas
Miss Prim and the Maverick Millionaire	Nina Singh
Their One Night Baby	Carol Marinelli
Forbidden to the Playboy Surgeon	Fiona Lowe
A Mother to Make a Family	Emily Forbes
The Nurse's Baby Secret	Janice Lynn
The Boss Who Stole Her Heart	Jennifer Taylor
Reunited by Their Pregnancy Surprise	Louisa Heaton
The Ten-Day Baby Takeover	Karen Booth
Expecting the Billionaire's Baby	Andrea Laurence

MILLS & BOON®
Large Print – April 2017

ROMANCE

A Di Sione for the Greek's Pleasure	Kate Hewitt
The Prince's Pregnant Mistress	Maisey Yates
The Greek's Christmas Bride	Lynne Graham
The Guardian's Virgin Ward	Caitlin Crews
A Royal Vow of Convenience	Sharon Kendrick
The Desert King's Secret Heir	Annie West
Married for the Sheikh's Duty	Tara Pammi
Winter Wedding for the Prince	Barbara Wallace
Christmas in the Boss's Castle	Scarlet Wilson
Her Festive Doorstep Baby	Kate Hardy
Holiday with the Mystery Italian	Ellie Darkins

HISTORICAL

Bound by a Scandalous Secret	Diane Gaston
The Governess's Secret Baby	Janice Preston
Married for His Convenience	Eleanor Webster
The Saxon Outlaw's Revenge	Elisabeth Hobbes
In Debt to the Enemy Lord	Nicole Locke

MEDICAL

Waking Up to Dr Gorgeous	Emily Forbes
Swept Away by the Seductive Stranger	Amy Andrews
One Kiss in Tokyo...	Scarlet Wilson
The Courage to Love Her Army Doc	Karin Baine
Reawakened by the Surgeon's Touch	Jennifer Taylor
Second Chance with Lord Branscombe	Joanna Neil

MILLS & BOON®

Why shop at millsandboon.co.uk?

Each year, thousands of romance readers find their perfect read at millsandboon.co.uk. That's because we're passionate about bringing you the very best romantic fiction. Here are some of the advantages of shopping at www.millsandboon.co.uk:

* **Get new books first**—you'll be able to buy your favourite books one month before they hit the shops

* **Get exclusive discounts**—you'll also be able to buy our specially created monthly collections, with up to 50% off the RRP

* **Find your favourite authors**—latest news, interviews and new releases for all your favourite authors and series on our website, plus ideas for what to try next

* **Join in**—once you've bought your favourite books, don't forget to register with us to rate, review and join in the discussions

Visit **www.millsandboon.co.uk**
for all this and more today!